Over 50

To Doris

OVER 50

Health & Happiness

Maureen McIntyre

MAUREEN MCINTYRE

Copyright © 2015 by Maureen McIntyre.

ISBN:	Softcover	978-1-5144-2391-2
	eBook	978-1-5144-2389-9

All rights reserved. No part of this book may be reproduced or transmitted in any form or by any means, electronic or mechanical, including photocopying, recording, or by any information storage and retrieval system, without permission in writing from the copyright owner.

This is a work of fiction. Names, characters, places and incidents either are the product of the author's imagination or are used fictitiously, and any resemblance to any actual persons, living or dead, events, or locales is entirely coincidental.

Any people depicted in stock imagery provided by Thinkstock are models, and such images are being used for illustrative purposes only. Certain stock imagery © Thinkstock.

Print information available on the last page.

Rev. date: 11/09/2015

To order additional copies of this book, contact:
Xlibris
1-888-795-4274
www.Xlibris.com
Orders@Xlibris.com
650615

DEDICATION

This book is dedicated to my family and friends.
A special thank you to Sandra for her editing skills.

Prologue

Joseph and I have been married for thirty-two years. We're both fifty-nine years young. I work as a receptionist in a doctor's office and Joe is an accountant for a large manufacturing company. I feel so lucky to have Joe in my life. When I was in university and running around with lots of different guys, I always hoped I would find a kind, thoughtful man. Of course at that age my priority was handsome and well built. I used to swoon over the football players and their tight bottoms. My thoughts are interrupted when Joe calls:

"Hey Maggie! Can you please help me hang the new picture we bought yesterday?"

"Sure Joe, be right there."

Joe and I had been to an auction sale the previous day and we both fell in love with a relaxing beach scene done in pastel shades. This picture reminds me of the time, just before we were married, when we stayed in a little, white cottage on Rice Lake. I remember the feelings of excitement just looking at my Joe and loving his arms around me. Of course the nights together were intoxicating and I couldn't imagine my life without him in it.

"I just have to have that picture in our bedroom so we see it first when we wake up," I said.

"I agree it's very beautiful and reminds me of our first trip to the cottage."

"Is this straight?" asked Joe as he held the picture up to the wall.

"A little to the left, Dear, and it will be perfect," I said.

After the picture was in its place on the wall and giving a very tranquil look to our room, Joe took me in his arms and gave me a big hug and then a kiss on the cheek. I still feel a tingle when Joe kisses me. We are still very much in love after all this time and three children later.

Joe and I have two sons, Peter and William and a daughter, Patricia. The boys are still single and in their twenties. Pat is thirty, married with a son, Robert, and a daughter, Marcia. Pat's husband, James, is thirty-two years old and a paediatrician. I am so happy our children are so successful. Guess we did something right.

Later this evening, Joe and I are supposed to go to visit friends to have a drink and play euchre. I just learned to play euchre two years ago. I figured since I'm getting older I should learn how to play cards because soon the active sports will be too difficult for this aging body. I love the game of euchre because it's easy and we can visit while we're playing it.

After dinner, we each got showered and dressed to go out.

"How does this outfit look?" I asked as I modelled my new black stretch pants (leggings) and royal blue sweater. I am so glad tight pants are in style right now. They are comfortable and I see men taking a second look when I am wearing them. I must say my tush isn't too bad at all. I exercise and walk a lot and I am quite proud of my body.

"You look beautiful, as always, Babe," Joe said.

I must admit I do look good in almost anything I wear as I am five foot five inches tall with a slim build. I have been blessed with dark curly hair and green eyes. I confess I do colour my hair now as there seems to be some grey in it. I have let my hair grow to shoulder length so I am able to put it up if I want to look more sophisticated. But tonight I will leave it down.

"Okay, Dear, I'll meet you downstairs," I called.

Joe and I live in a lovely, but very large, two-storey red brick house near the city limits. It was a perfect place to bring up a family but is starting to feel too big for two people. Several of our friends have down-sized and I'm starting to think this might be the answer for us. I feel tired just going up and down the stairs so many times each day.

The gardening and housework are starting to feel overwhelming even though I have a cleaning lady every two weeks. I still have to do the bathrooms and kitchen in between her visits. I can't stand to see a dirty kitchen. Too fussy maybe, but that's just the way I am. Can't teach an old dog new tricks so they say.

At nearly sixty years of age, both Joe and I are starting to notice the stairs becoming a bit of a challenge. Joe's left hip bothers him, on occasion, as he suffers from osteoarthritis. The stairs certainly don't help his condition.

In about twenty minutes Joe and I are on our way to our good friends' house to play cards.

Chapter 1

"Please come in," said Joan as she answered the door. "How are you both tonight?"

"Just fine Joan," I said. "And how are you and Ian?" I asked as Ian arrived at the door.

"Good evening Joe and Maggie," Ian said while extending his arm to shake Joe's hand. He then gave me a kiss on the cheek. "We're so happy you could join us for euchre tonight. We've been busy all day and it will be nice to relax for a while."

Joan and Ian have been our good friends since our university days. We married around the same time and started our families shortly after. I feel that Joan is more like a sister. I can tell her anything and she will listen. Joan shares everything with me as well, like last year when she found a lump in her right breast. She was terrified to tell Ian. We kept it to ourselves for a few days and I took Joan to the doctor. Thank God she was okay; no cancer, just a small cyst.

We played cards for about two hours when Joan said, "what is trump for this hand? I've forgotten. I must be getting tired. I think it's time to stop and have a coffee and some of the banana bread I made this afternoon."

"Sounds good to me."

I was starting to feel a little peckish as well and Joan makes the best banana bread I have ever tasted. She's an excellent cook.

Everyone moved to the kitchen and I helped Joan with the coffee and goodies while the men made themselves comfortable at the table. Soon we joined our husbands.

"You know, we are thinking about taking a holiday for a couple of weeks, to Cuba. Why don't you two join us?" said Ian.

"That could be fun. When are you planning to go?" I asked, rather excitedly. Joan said "in a couple of weeks if we can find a good trip." I looked at Joe and he agreed that we could also use a holiday.

We usually go away once or twice a year but this year we have both been busy at work and what with Joe's arthritis acting up through the winter, we have been at home. I love to travel. Now that we are getting older I think it's important to travel as much as possible. You never know when one of us could come down with a health problem preventing us from travelling, or raising the insurance to an unacceptable level. So I'm quite excited to be able to travel with our very good friends. This could be a lot of fun and God knows I need some fun. I have been feeling a little depressed from not getting away for a while. I really hope this trip works out.

Two weeks later we were all in Cayo Santa Maria, Cuba. We enjoyed the sea, the beach and the pool. Joan and I were talking one afternoon as we sat by the pool.

"We are booked for the specialty Italian restaurant tomorrow night. Why don't you and Ian join us for dinner?"

"Let's go to the reception desk and see if they still have room," Joan remarked. As we walked to the desk in the main building we were talking and laughing. "What a great vacation," said Joan. "I agree we needed this after working so hard."

At La Trattoria, the next evening we enjoyed lobster bisque, bread for dipping, penne in brandy sauce, a Mediterranean salad and for dessert, tiramisu.

I just love Italian food; I sometimes think I should have been born in Italy. The Mediterranean diet has to be the healthiest diet in the world with so many fresh ingredients. I always try to cook this way for Joe and myself. Maybe at this restaurant I can pick up some tips for a new recipe.

"When we get home from this vacation we are going to look around for a smaller home. Now that the kids are grown we no longer need the big house," Ian commented. Joe said "You know, I've been thinking along those lines lately as well. The stairs are starting to be a challenge with my arthritic hip." "Joe, I didn't know you felt that way," I said. "Well I haven't mentioned it but it has been on my mind. What do you think of downsizing?" "I would be willing to look at something smaller when we get home."

"You know," Joan said, "there are some nice communities for the fifty plus age group. They are less work with no gardening or snow shovelling. They have activities that you can join and they go on outings from time to time. Maybe we can look into something like that?" I agree, Joan, this could be just what we need."

I thought to myself, I'll research the fifty plus communities when we get back home. Gee, I'm starting to feel excited for this new venture. Maybe, when we retire, we can learn some new activities. Retirement no longer sounds like grandma sitting in a rocking chair all day. We are going to be able to remain active. This makes me feel very good.

This could be fun. "Joe, what do you think about such a community?" "I agree it could be a good move for us too."

The next day Joe and I went on a Jeep tour of the island while Joan and Ian spent the day at the pool.

Joe and I met three other couples in the lobby. We were all around the same age. There were six other groups which seemed to be divided according to their ages as well. Our guide came over and introduced himself as Marco and he told us he would be with us all day even when we stopped at a local restaurant for lunch. We followed Marco outside and there were seven Jeeps lined up. We were walked to the third one and we all climbed in the back. These Jeeps had two bench seats, one on each side of the Jeep. We sat four people on each side. The seats were made of wood and I thought I was going to have a pretty sore bum by the end of the day.

Marco took off at precisely ten o'clock. All the Jeeps followed in a long line until we got away from the resort. Then we divided to take different routes. I guessed this was why we were grouped according to our age. The two Jeeps with younger people in them went up a mountain, over a lot of bumps. They were all standing up, making a lot of noise, singing and yelling. Boy, I'm glad I wasn't in one of those Jeeps. Marco was taking it a little easier with us. We took a path that gave us a perfect view of the water. It was lovely and I was so glad that my small camera was hooked to my belt. I took lots of pictures.

At twelve noon all seven Jeeps met at an outside restaurant for lunch. They served us grilled chicken, salad, roasted potatoes. There were lots of cool drinks and ice cream for dessert. This restaurant has been approved by our resort so it was safe for us to eat here. We all appreciated the ice cream as the temperature that day was in the high eighties. After lunch and the inevitable line at the ladies washroom, I am sure that ladies rooms have been designed by men as there is always a long lineup to get in. Men can pee in the urinal and even share it with another if necessary. We need a stall each and some ladies take a long time fiddling with their clothes. Eventually we all got through the line and returned to our Jeeps. Going back, Marco took a much bumpier route through the trees and up and down hills. Oh boy! My bum hurts now. I can shift from cheek to cheek as most of us are doing but it isn't helping much. A cushion would have been a nice touch.

We arrived back at the resort at four o'clock, tired and sore but happy at what we had seen on the trip. It was very good but not something I would be in a hurry to repeat. When we get home I'll put my pictures on the computer and delete the ones I don't like. Praise for the computer.

Now it's time for a shower and a very welcomed rest before dinner.

That evening at dinner, Joe was a little fidgety and at the show later on he kept getting up from his chair and going for a short walk. "What's wrong?" I asked. "I think that Jeep ride was a little too much for my hip. It hurts when I sit in one place; it seems better to walk a little." "Do you have any medication with you?" "Yes, but it's back in the room, I'll take it before bed. Don't worry, Dear, I'm fine." "Okay, as soon as the show is over we can retire for the night." The show was excellent and we all enjoyed it but at 10:30 we returned to our respective rooms with a plan to meet again for breakfast the next day. "Joe, are you sure you are okay? You know they have a doctor here at the resort if you would like to see him." "I'll be fine, it was just the bumpy ride in the Jeep. Please don't worry about me." "Okay," I lied. I always worry when something is wrong with Joe or one of the kids. Women's prerogative, I guess.

"Would you like a cup of tea and a cookie? I bought some today when I visited the Gift Shop." "I'd love tea and a cookie and I'll take my arthritis medication at the same time." "Would you like me to find us a movie on television and we can sit at the table and enjoy our tea?" Joe asked. "Sounds good to me," I replied, happy that he seemed to be okay. "I think I'll get ready for bed first." "Okay Honey, I'll find the movie."

The next morning, feeling rested and in no more pain, Joe and I met Joan and Ian at the breakfast buffet to start another day of sun and fun at the resort.

"We are going on the shopping tour today. It goes to a small town where we'll see how cigars are made. Then we go to a pottery place. We'll see how all their lovely pots and vases are formed and painted. Then we go into the store where we can purchase something if we like. I'm looking forward to this tour," Joan said. "Why don't you join us?" Ian added. "Joe and I are just having a quiet day today. I think we'll be on the beach most of the day. We'll meet you at 6:30 for a drink before dinner. Have a good day, you two." "Thanks and you have a good day too," Joan responded.

I know Joe needs to rest today. Heck, even my bum is sore and I don't have problems with arthritis. A day on the beach will feel very good after being bounced around all over Hell's half acre yesterday.

After breakfast, Joan and Ian left for their tour. Joe and I went back to our room to change into bathing suits for a day on the beach. "Maggie, thanks for being so patient last night when I wasn't feeling too well," Joe said. "You're welcome Dear, I'm glad you're feeling better today." Joe put his arms around me and gave me a big bear hug. We gave each other a kiss on the lips and hugged a little tighter.

I always feel butterflies in my tummy when Joe kisses me like this. After all these years you would think I would have grown up, but I'm still like a giddy teenager. Actually, I hope it never changes.

"If you are intending to go to the beach, I think we better stop what we're doing or in a minute we'll not be going anywhere," Joe quietly remarked.

"Okay Dear, let's get changed and go to the beach. Could you please put this suntan lotion on my back before we go out?" "Sure and then would you please do my back too?" "Do you have my e-reader in the beach bag?" I don't take my reader to the beach as I find it is too difficult to read in the sunlight. Instead I have two good books that I can read outside. "Yes Dear, I have your reader and my book and also our sunglasses." "Honey don't forget to wear a hat as the sun is very hot here."

Joe and I spent several hours on the beach. We walked along the shoreline and gathered shells. I feel so comfortable and happy walking hand in hand with Joe along the beach gathering shells and stones. The feeling is like nothing else on earth; so relaxing.

Then we sat under an umbrella for a while reading our respective books. After a couple of hours in the sun, Joe suggested that we go for a swim to cool off. I readily agreed as I was feeling quite drained from the heat. At lunchtime, we decided to just go to the bar on the beach. We could go to that bar in our bathing suits. I have a lovely wrap that matches my suit so I am anxious to wear it to lunch. When we got to the bar we checked out the menu. It was mostly fast food, pizza, fries, hot dogs and hamburgers. We both decided on a hot dog and a light beer. This seems perfect for a lunch on the beach. I think I could spend the rest of my life like this, it feels so wonderful.

By about 4 o'clock, a shower and air-conditioned room were sounding very inviting. When we entered our room Joe took me in his arms and started kissing me. Of course, I reciprocated with pleasure. Why am I so lucky to have a perfect husband? We made love for what seemed a very short time but when I looked at the clock, it had been forty-five minutes and then I got up to shower as Joe had fallen asleep. By the time I had showered and washed my hair, Joe was awake and ready to shower as well. I selected a pair of white skinny pants and a lovely soft pink flowing blouse. I added white sandals with a small heel and I felt very sexy. Joe was impressed. "Maggie my beautiful wife, I love you." "I love you too; you always make me feel special." Joe makes me feel so loved. He's always complimenting me and I must say I look forward to his adoration.

At 6:30 we were all together again for a pre-dinner drink. "How was your tour?" I asked Joan. "It was a lot of fun. We watched a local man make pottery. He started with a lump of clay and spun it on a wheel. When it was formed into a pot he sent it to dry and took another one that had already dried, so he could paint it. The paint he used was all from berries and fruits, all natural colours. He did a beautiful job painting the pot and then he added a glaze. I was very impressed." "How was your day of rest?" "Great, thanks Joan. We spent most of the day on the beach."

By 7 o'clock we were all very hungry and we proceeded to the buffet for dinner. Tonight the menu included Mahi Mahi fish. "I love this fish and I think I'll have it with some rice and a few vegetables." "That sounds good," replied Joan. "I think I'll have the same." Joe and Ian wanted something more filling so they went for the beef stew and both of them added pasta to their dish. Sitting at the table, we discussed plans for tomorrow. "I want to take the salsa class at the pool," said Joan. "And I like the Spanish lesson at 11 a.m.," I said. I've taken Spanish lessons before and I'm able to speak enough to get directions or to buy something.

Ian and Joe decided to play shuffleboard. "We can meet at the beach restaurant for lunch at 12:30," I said. All agreed. "And why don't we spend the afternoon at the pool." "There's going to be a good show tonight. The resort has hired some professional dancers to come and there will also be a few jokes told, in English, I hope, as my Spanish is a little rusty," Joe commented.

At the beach restaurant at 12:30, the four of us sat together talking about downsizing our homes. We were all very interested in exploring the possibility of living in a community for active seniors. There were two such villages in the vicinity we had chosen. "Well, when we get home why don't we go together to view these properties and that way we can get each other's opinion on the area and the homes," I said. "Okay," replied Ian. Joan was also in agreement. Of course Joe would do anything for me so that wasn't a problem. I'm getting quite excited about a fifty plus community. After I do my research I will have more answers as to what is available to the residents.

At the end of a couple of wonderful weeks in the sun and sand we had to return to reality and to begin our search for new homes.

Chapter 2

"I've set up appointments for us with Village #1 for Friday evening, after we all get home from work," said Joan. "We can meet at their on-site office at seven thirty. Hope this is okay with you?" "Yes Joan," I replied. "We'll see you there."

I'm starting to get very excited about the possibilities ahead for us. Joe and I both like to be active; we are not the type to sit around doing virtually nothing. I can't wait to see what activities we are able to join.

Friday was a busy day in the doctor's office but I couldn't keep my thoughts off the exciting meeting that night. "I'd love to live in an area with lots of activities instead of always having to drive to the gym, cards and tennis. It would be great to be able to walk to my activities."

At exactly 7:30, Joe and I met Joan and Ian and Mrs. Booth, the sales representative for Village #1. "I've lined up four different homes for you to see tonight. We'll start with a condo unit, then a townhouse, and then I have a semi-detached house and a single dwelling."

The condo was lovely with two bedrooms, two bathrooms and a den that could be used as an office. "I must say I really like this but I'm not sure it would be big enough after living in such a large house for so many years." Mrs. Booth then offered the townhouse. "I don't like the fact that there are no windows at either side of the house as it is attached on both sides. Maybe an end unit would be better," said Joan.

"Then let's go to the semi-detached and the single home," offered Mrs. Booth. Both of these homes were nice and were suitable for either Joe and me or Joan and Ian. Then we went to look at the activity centre. There was a tennis court and shuffleboard outside. The pool was also outside which limited its use to summertime. When we entered the building we saw many different rooms used for different activities. "There's certainly enough to do here," I said. "Yes we have fifty three different activities and all are available to our residents free of charge." "We will think about it and get back to you soon. And thank you for your time," said Joe.

Back at our house over coffee, Joan commented, "I don't like the fact that there is no indoor pool. I like to swim for exercise and the wintertime is when I need it the most." I feel the same way. I love to swim in the winter when there is snow all around and I'm in a nice warm pool looking out.

"I wasn't too impressed with the kitchen in either the semi-detached or single home. I think it's too small," I complained. "Oh Maggie, you're just so used to our big kitchen that anything would look small to you now," said Joe. "Maybe so, but I spend a lot of time in the kitchen and it will be even more time when I retire. I really think I have to love it." Joan agreed and so we all decided to try Village #2. I offered to set up the appointment for us. "When would you like to go?" "We're free Wednesday evening if that suits you," Ian said. Joe replied, "That would be fine with us too. Okay Maggie, you may go ahead and make the arrangements for Wednesday at 7:30 again."

Joan seems a little quiet tonight, I wonder what is wrong.

"Joan, is something wrong? Are you having second thoughts about moving?"

"Oh no Maggie, I'm just a little concerned about Ian."

"Is Ian not well?"

"Oh, it's nothing like that but I think he might be having an affair. He goes out mysteriously. He says he is working but if I call his office there is never an answer."

"Try not to worry Joan; I'm sure Ian isn't cheating on you. Just wait, you'll see."

When Wednesday finally arrived, we met James at Village #2. The houses were nice; similar to the last village but this site had an advantage over the first site already in that the pool was indoors and the kitchens in the houses were open concept and much larger than Village #1. I'm starting to feel that maybe this village will be our new home. It looks beautiful with well-manicured gardens.

When James showed us the Clubhouse, he said, "we have eighty-six different activities for you to enjoy. There is a social club here and they arrange outings for everyone. We have tennis, golf, shuffleboard and bocce just to mention a few and if there is something you would like to do and we don't offer it, just speak to the President and arrangements will be made if there are enough interested people. "This village sounds like what we are looking for," I said.

After the tour, Joan suggested we go to the coffee shop to talk. I was quite excited about this Village # 2 and Joe was on board also but Joan and Ian seemed less enthusiastic. "I think we would prefer something a little more private that we can look after ourselves because in the village all outside maintenance is done for you." "We enjoy working in the garden. I think we just need a smaller house and garden to make us happy." "Would you like Joe and me to help you find a house that would suit your needs?" I asked. "Yes, thank you, that would be great," replied Joan. Ian said he would set up some appointments and let us know. We agreed and we all left for home as we have work tomorrow.

We visited a number of smaller houses and Joan and Ian finally found one that they liked. They put their conditional offer in on the house. Joe and I have chosen a lovely semi-detached home in Village #2. We're putting an offer in on this house tomorrow. It's been a long time since we have been involved with real estate. We've been in our present house for many years and the three children were born and brought up in it. This is a big decision for us and I feel a little sad at selling our family home. I do realize that this is the best decision as we are getting older and Joe is having problems keeping up with the yard work.

After one month of house showings, Joan and Ian sold their house and firmed up their offer. Our house sold a week later. Now we were moving! Hope this is the right thing to do. I think I'll be losing a lot of sleep over this. I'm a worrier; wish I wasn't but I have always been this way so I hardly think I will change anytime soon. Here come sleepless nights!

"Isn't this exciting!" exclaimed Joan as we packed the breakables from Joan's china cabinet. "It sure is and next month we are doing mine, I said. Can't wait. We're both starting new lives and I hope our choices work out well for us all." "Oh I'm sure we have done the right thing. These big houses are getting to be too much to look after at our age." "Where should I put this box Joan, it's full now?" "Please mark it breakable and put it in the corner, thanks." "When we finish the dining room we can start on the kitchen," Joan said. "Okay Joan but we should leave a few dishes out as you don't move until next week." "Good idea Mags, I guess we'll have to eat during the next week." We worked tirelessly and finished the dining room and kitchen. The movers were going to take care of the rest.

"Let's have a glass of wine before we join the men for dinner at Chicken Chalet," offered Joan. "That sounds great," I said as I held the 2 wine glasses we had not packed and Joan poured Castelli Romani, an Italian red wine. Both of us enjoyed a quiet half hour before dinner. We had worked so hard and I was feeling tired. I'm really looking forward to that glass of wine and a half hour to relax before we meet the men.

After dinner we went back to our house for a game of euchre as we had another month before our move and the house was still intact. "Maggie and I will help you unpack the day after your move," offered Joe. "Thanks Joe, Joan and I would be happy to do the same for you next month." "All settled then," said Joe.

Our plans had been made; no turning back now. Boy! I hope we're doing the right thing.

The following week Joan and Ian moved into their smaller home. The move went well and the unpacking the next day was quick with four people helping. Joan and I took care of the dining room and the kitchen as these items were breakable. The men looked after moving the furniture into the correct location.

Chapter 3

This is midweek and I am driving home from work enjoying the songs on the radio.

Hey! That car in front of me looks a lot like Ian's car. But I'm sure Ian is out of town on business. It can't be Ian as there are two people in the car and I know Joan is still at work because she phoned me before I left the office. I'm going to try to see if it's Ian. I'll pull up beside him in the other lane. I don't want him to recognize me so I think I should just follow him. I'll take down the license number and check later. I'm pretty sure it is Ian, but who's with him?

Oh no! A red light. There goes Ian and the mystery woman. I wonder if I should tell Joan what I've seen. Joan has confided in me so I must tell her, but I'll check the license first so I don't stir up trouble where it doesn't exist. When I tell Joan, her suspicions are confirmed.

The following month, Joan and I packed up our house and the move took place as scheduled.

"Joe, where would you like your favourite chair placed in the family room? The movers put it in the corner where I had planned to put the lamp table." "Over on the far wall would be great so I can watch T.V. but don't you move it. Wait for me to come and help you." "Okay Dear." "The house is starting to come together well, don't you think?" "Yes, it's starting to look like home." "Tomorrow I think we should take a walk around the Village and get a little bit familiar with the area," I suggested. "Good idea," agreed Joe. "Then maybe next week we can check into some of the activities offered here." "Sounds like fun," I agreed. I can't wait to find out what activities we're going to be able to choose from. I think I'll try a few out and then pick the ones I like the best. I know, since I'm still working, that I can't do everything but I'd really like to start to become involved. I've always liked to be busy and I know living here, I can keep myself out of mischief.

The following week Joe joined the Putting Club and the Wood Carving Class. I signed up for Aquafit which was offered three mornings a week. I'll be able to go before work. We both would have liked to take the ballroom dancing class but with Joe's arthritic hip we decided not to participate at this time. Hopefully, in the future, we'll have the opportunity to join. Joe is thinking that when he retires he'll probably have his hip replaced. It seems that a number of our friends find themselves in a similar position. It's the age, I guess. Getting old is difficult but it beats the alternative.

Chapter 4

One evening after dinner as we were sitting in the lanai, with a cup of coffee, and just relaxing after a busy day, the phone rang.

"Shall I get that Maggie?" asked Joe.

"It's okay Dear, I was about to go in to get a magazine so I can answer it."

"Thanks Honey."

As I walked through the kitchen I picked up the phone.

"Hello."

"Hello, may I please speak to Margaret Henderson?"

"This is Maggie, can I help you?"

"I'm your neighbour Barb Williams. Sam and I live two doors down from you. We're having some of the neighbours on our street for a barbeque on Saturday evening. We would love it if you and your husband could join us."

"We would love to and thank you."

"See you around six o'clock," said Barb.

"Can I bring something?" I offered, thinking about my favourite salad that everyone loves. Maybe it's because of the almonds or the Feta cheese but more likely it's the chick peas. Anyway it's a very popular salad. I also make my own secret recipe oil and vinegar dressing; very tasty.

"No, but thanks for offering."

"Thanks again, see you at six."

I hung up the phone and grabbed my magazine and headed back outside to tell Joe.

"We have just been invited to a barbeque on Saturday at our neighbours. I accepted for us, hope that's okay Dear?"

"Of course, it's great. We'll be able to meet some of our new neighbours. I look forward to that."

Saturday came and I put on new white pants with a black cotton blouse and white wedge sandals. I always love to get dressed up; it's half the fun of going out.

"How do I look Dear?"

"Beautiful as ever, Honey."

Joe decided to match me and he put on white shorts and a black tee. I still find Joe extremely sexy and tonight is no exception. He looks wonderful in black and white. Joe has such nice legs that I encourage him to wear shorts often.

"I'm excited to meet some of our new neighbours," Joe exclaimed.

"Me too."

Joe and I arrived at the home of neighbours Barb and Sam with a bottle of red wine and a small potted Gerbera daisy in bright red. Barb was very thankful but said it wasn't necessary. I know that, but I don't like to go to someone's home empty handed and a flower and bottle of wine is really nothing.

A few of the guests were already there and Barb introduced us to them. As more people arrived, more introductions were made. Everyone was friendly and very welcoming.

I thought there must be some scandals and/or affairs in a community of this size. I'm sure I'll hear about them soon. I'm going to keep my ears open tonight to learn as much as I can about our neighbours.

"May I help you put out the condiments and salads?" I offered.

"That would be nice, thank you. We're just putting everything outside on the picnic table by the barbeque. The men are doing the cooking. We have hamburgers, steaks and chicken wings and breasts. Hope you and Joe enjoy our choices."

"It sounds just perfect, Barb. Looks like you have gone to a lot of trouble."

"Not really, we enjoy doing this once a year for our neighbours. It helps to make for a friendly street. Here in the Community we like to help each other so it helps to know something about the people who live close by."

"Be careful what you tell Sarah though, she likes to talk about everybody. Maybe being nosey is her m.o." I knew it! There is scandal in this village. Things are getting more exciting all the time. I like to be part of the in-crowd but I draw the line at spreading rumours. They just come back to bite you. I, however, have no problem with listening. In fact, I enjoy hearing the gossip. Does that make me a bad person? I hope not.

With everyone helping each other as we age, I think Joe and I are going to love living here. All the guests have gone out of their way to make us feel welcome and I really do appreciate it but I'm thinking I'll keep our business private. I don't want our new neighbours knowing everything about us, at least not yet. We have nothing to hide but a little privacy is always good.

The barbeque was a big success and Joe and I met several people all of whom were happy to include us in their conversations.

I learned that there is a Ladies Social Group in the Community and Sue invited me to the next meeting.

"We meet once a month and plan outings, trips, theatre, shows, casino trips and other fun things. We also plan lunches where four ladies go out together and get to know each other better. We are allowed to take our spouses on the trips if they would like to go but not to the meetings or lunches. There's a meeting on Monday morning at ten o'clock and we could go together if you wish." I mentally review my calendar and I remember that the doctor has a meeting out of town on Monday, so it will not be a problem for me to take the morning off.

"I think that would be wonderful. I could meet you at nine forty-five at your house."

"Okay, it's a plan."

As we were about to put out the dessert, one of the men (Gordon) was standing by himself close to a tree in the garden. I noticed that he looked a little pale. When I started over to see if he would like a drink, I noticed that he looked as if he was staring into space. At the same time, Matt also noticed Gordon and he hurried to his side and we eased Gordon to the ground as he lost consciousness. Matt knew that Gordon was a diabetic so he offered him some orange juice and he slowly came around. Because Gordon lives alone, Matt called 911 and he was taken to the hospital. I can now see how knowing your neighbours well could save a life. What a wonderful arrangement this is for everyone in this community. Looking out for each other works as we age and develop all sorts of conditions that could require someone's assistance.

The barbeque was fun and lasted until about two in the morning with singing of old tunes and drinking wine. No one had to drive home as they were all close neighbours. So we were able to enjoy the wine without worry.

The next morning, Gordon called Barb and told her it was just a mix up in his insulin and after being stabilized he was discharged from the hospital. Barb phoned all the guests who were at the barbeque to let them know that Gordon was okay. We all appreciated the news.

On Sunday, the day following the barbeque, I couldn't stop thinking about Matt, the man who ran to Gordon's aid. Matt was tall, slim and handsome. He had been a widower for four years since he lost his wife to cancer. I was mentally reviewing all my friends and acquaintances to see if there was anyone suitable for this very attractive gentleman. Matt seemed rather lost and lonely when I met him last night. I'm not normally a match maker but there was just something about this man that tugged at my heart strings. Since I'm so happy with my marriage to Joe, I want everyone to be as happy. I started thinking of my friends, work mates and acquaintances. I can't think of anyone off hand but I'll keep trying. I hate to see the sadness in his eyes when he speaks about his wife. He must have loved her very deeply. I can't imagine the pain he must be going through. After talking to him I'm sure he would love to have a companion, a woman to take to dinner or a show. It's difficult doing some things alone especially when you have always had a spouse on your arm. I really hope I can help.

Chapter 5

Joe and I slept in until ten the next morning.

"Would you like to go to the market today, Dear?" I suggested as I poured two cups of coffee and buttered some toast. "I could use some fresh vegetables to make a special soup. I just got a new recipe and I can't wait to try it. We also need fruit as we only have a few grapes left and two bananas."

At the market we were able to get everything we needed and more. Joe bought a bouquet of beautiful pink carnations for me to put on the table in the lanai. I love to have fresh flowers in the house as they just make me feel happy. Carnations last a long time so we will have the memory of our trip to the market for quite a while. We both really love going to the market. They have so much that we can't get in the grocery store. There is much more than just fruit and vegetables. They have home baking and they sell all sorts of thing like hats, gloves, belts, kitchen gadgets. I love pawing through anything for the kitchen to see if there is something I don't have. If I don't have it, I probably don't need it but that never stopped me before so I will probably buy it now too. My problem is finding a place to put all of these utensils when I get them home. I am trying to keep my small appliances to a minimum because I now have limited storage space and I like to keep the counters fairly clear for preparing food.

Back at home later that day, I started searching my closet for something nice to wear tomorrow for my first meeting at the Ladies Social Club. I chose navy Capri pants and a loose, flowing, blue top. As I returned to the living room, Joe was pouring our drinks. The popcorn was already on the coffee table and the movie ready to start.

I'm quite excited to go to the Ladies Club tomorrow and luckily I have the morning off. The doctor I work for is going to a convention and he told me to take the morning off. Hopefully I will meet some more ladies here in the Community.

"I'm sure you will enjoy it, Honey, and don't worry about me. I have a meeting at work tomorrow morning but I'll be home for lunch."

The next morning we went our separate ways. I enjoyed the meeting and learned there was a trip planned, in two weeks' time, to go on a boat cruise and husbands were invited as well. We will meet at the tour bus which will take us to the boat. Joe and I decided to go on this trip.

The day of the trip soon arrived. When Joe got up that morning he could barely walk; his hip was causing extreme pain and it seemed to be locked. Joe had played golf the day before and instead of using a golf cart as he usually does, he decided to walk for the exercise. This was obviously too much for Joe's arthritic hip. Since we had already paid for the trip, Joe told me to go with them and he would stay home and rest. I wasn't sure this was such a good idea as Joe isn't one to sit and rest. I also feel a little strange going on this trip without Joe even though I know some of the ladies who are going. Joe insisted and wouldn't take no for an answer, so I conceded.

"Okay, but you know it won't be as much fun without you," I said.

"Just enjoy yourself Honey. I'll be fine. I think I'll just catch up on some reading."

"Do you have a good book or would you like me to go to the library for you?"

"Thanks Honey but I have two new books and an instruction manual for the gazebo I promised to assemble for Pat and James next weekend."

"Okay Dear, have a good day but be sure to rest your hip."

"I will Honey. See you at dinner time." I'm not sure I can trust Joe to rest but what choice do I have.

Sue and Jack offered to take me with them to catch the bus.

"Wow! Look at the size of that boat," I said in astonishment. I had expected something much smaller. This boat could accommodate four hundred and fifty people. It had seats and tables and a cafeteria on the main deck where we are going to have lunch. On the upper deck there were sun chairs and tables with umbrellas to use when the boat was travelling to its destination. There was even a bar that served wine, beer and spirits and also water, juice and soda. There was a cute boutique where we could purchase souvenirs. I was very impressed. I have never been on a cruise before so this was a real treat. I wish Joe was here with me as he would really enjoy it.

By the time we boarded the boat, it was eleven-thirty, almost lunchtime. Sue and Jack had already invited me to sit with them but then Sue spotted Matt sitting alone and she invited him to join our group as well. Matt graciously accepted the offer. I'm happy that Sue did this because it gives me a chance to get to know Matt a little better and maybe I can think of someone he would like to meet. Besides I feel very much alone with Joe not being here and almost everyone else is in couples.

"How are you and Joe enjoying the Community so far?" Matt asked.

"We love it, thanks; everyone is so friendly it's as if we've known them all our lives," I politely replied. I hope Matt can't tell how attractive I think he is. I could feel myself starting to blush and hope that it's not noticeable. After all I'm happily married to Joe and we're still very much in love. Why am I blushing just because he's good looking? Heaven knows I have met a lot of good looking men over the years but my body has never betrayed me like this before.

"I'm sorry Joe's not feeling well but I must be honest. You look stunning today and I'm honoured to join you for lunch."

"Thank you Matt, but you embarrass me."

Sue and Jack looked at each other and winked. They could see the attraction and Sue did notice the blush earlier. Of course, when we were alone, she had to mention it and this only made it worse. "Sue please!"

"After lunch would anyone care to join me on the upper deck to catch some rays?" Sue suggested. As soon as I accepted, Matt was eager to join us and so Jack consented as well. Jack had a good mystery novel with him. He very seldom went anywhere without a book.

Sue and I donned our bathing suits and headed for the upper deck and four lounge chairs. Matt was already there wearing a pair of cargo shorts and a red tee. He had secured four chairs together. Matt had also managed to find four lounge cushions. He was very thoughtful. As we approached, Matt stood up to offer us seats.

"Hi," I said, and when Matt looked up to respond, the look on his face told a whole new story. I have seen men look at me with appreciation in the past but this time it was way beyond anything I've seen before. Oh no! There's that blush again.

"Hi yourself," he politely responded. "Choose a seat. Jack has gone to get four bottles of water."

Sue deliberately chose the third and fourth chairs for herself and Jack, leaving the chair next to Matt for me. She was not trying to cause trouble; she just knew that we would enjoy each other's company which we did for about an hour. Then we all decided it was time to get out of the sun and go inside for a snack before the cruise was over.

Chapter 6

When I returned home I found Joe lying on the couch in a great deal of pain. I don't think he has moved very much today at all.

"Oh Dear, you look awful. Have you taken any of your medication?"

"Yes," replied Joe in a soft, quiet voice. "I took two pills every four hours but they didn't help, so a couple of hours ago I took two acetaminophen with codeine. I feel very weak but the pain is still there."

"Can you walk to the car if I help you? I think we should go the Emergency Department."

"I feel dizzy but if I can hold your arm, I think I can make it."

"Okay, would you like a sweater?"

"No thanks, I'm fine."

I put the car seat straight up as this was the most comfortable position for Joe.

In ten minutes we were at the local hospital.

"Just wait in the car Dear, I'll go inside and get a wheelchair for you."

"Okay Honey," Joe reluctantly agreed. As he waited for Maggie, Joe thought: I have never been sick before and it makes me feel helpless to have Maggie taking care of me. I should be taking care of her.

"Okay, I'll help you get out of the car. The brake is on the chair so you can sit right down."

Joe was still in a considerable amount of pain so he would have done anything he was asked to do at this point.

We entered Triage and were quickly taken to a bed as there were not too many people there at this particular time. It was dinnertime for most. I have heard that sometimes you have to wait in Emerg for several hours before you are seen by a doctor. I was expecting a wait so I am pleased that we were taken in quickly. I hate to see Joe suffering and I can't help with this one.

The Emergency Department physician summoned the orthopaedic surgeon who was "on call" and then ordered a pain killer to be administered intravenously. This medication is starting to take effect as the orthopaedic surgeon is arriving. I think I will have to help Joe answer the questions as he is starting to slur his words and he's not making too much sense at the moment.

"Hello Mr. Henderson, I am Dr. Chalmers. What seems to be the problem?"

"When I got up this morning my left hip seemed to be locked. After walking around it felt better but then the pain started." Joe is doing pretty well explaining his problem to the doctor but I'll stay in case he needs my help.

As Joe related his experience, Dr. Chalmers could see the pain on his face.

"Did you take anything?" the doctor asked.

"Yes, I have medication for my arthritis and I took two pills every four hours all day. By early afternoon there was still no relief so I took two acetaminophen with codeine but even that didn't help the pain."

"Did you feel any effects from the medication?"

"Yes, it made me light headed and I was afraid to walk alone."

"How are you feeling now after the medication the nurse gave you? It should be just starting to take effect."

"Much better thank you, a little less pain and I feel a little giddy, which is kind of nice."

"Okay Mr. Henderson, I will give you a prescription for something stronger than what you have been taking and I'd like to see you in my office next week. The nurse will give you an appointment before you leave. You can fill the prescription at the hospital pharmacy but please use the wheelchair for your safety. It was nice to meet you, Mr. and Mrs. Henderson, and I will see you next week."

When the day of the appointment arrived I said, "let me drive you to the doctor's office. I know the medication you're on is strong."

"Thank you Honey," Joe replied rather thankful that he didn't have to battle the traffic with his reflexes being slower than normal.

"Please come in Mr. and Mrs. Henderson. Dr. Chalmers will see you in a minute."

"Thank you."

When Dr. Chalmers came into the room he asked Joe a number of questions and then he said, "Mr. Henderson I feel you could benefit from a left hip replacement." Dr. Chalmers described the surgery, benefits and rehabilitation. He also explained the risks. "Any time a general anesthetic is used there are certain risks. Mr. Henderson you are otherwise healthy, therefore the risks are minimal. I will give you a few minutes to discuss this proposal with your wife while I see a patient in the next room."

"Thank you Doctor," uttered Joe very nervously.

Since Joe has been suffering with this hip for a long time now and things are starting to worsen, both of us decided it was time for the surgery.

The doctor returned and Joe said, "I feel I should have something definitive done and so my wife and I have agreed to the left hip replacement."

"I think you have made the right decision Mr. Henderson and my receptionist will book an appointment for you. Speak to her on your way out."

"Thank you again, Doctor."

The surgery was booked for three weeks in the future.

"That will give me time to mentally prepare myself for my first surgery," Joe remarked to me on the way home.

"I know you're nervous but I'm sure you'll be fine. The doctor has done many of these procedures and as long as you follow his instructions for rest and rehabilitation, I don't think you have anything to worry about."

"Thanks Honey, for trying to reassure me."

The next week Joe and I accepted an invitation from our friends, Joan and Ian, to go to their new home for a barbeque and a game of euchre. It might be a few weeks before Joe will be able to go out visiting after his surgery. I think it will help take his mind off the procedure. I know he's worried, even though he won't admit it. I feel him tossing and turning at night and I know he's not getting his proper sleep. Last night I made a pot of Camomile tea to relax him and help him sleep. I think he slept a little better because I didn't wake as many times to his rolling around, as often happens, and his stealing of all the covers. Sometimes I have to get up and grab another blanket. I prefer this to waking him up when he finally falls asleep.

"How do you like your new house?" I asked. I've been there before but now that they're settled in I want to know if they are happy with the choice they made.

"It's great not having as much to clean. We're able to go out shopping or to a show during the week. Ian is quite happy too with his garden. He has tomatoes, peppers, zucchini, and all sorts of herbs. Remind me before you leave to pick some vegetables for you to take home with you. Ian really enjoys gardening. How are you and Joe making out in your new home?"

"We're happy too. We don't have a garden but we do have herbs in the lanai. We've met a lot of very nice people. Everyone seems so friendly. There is however one exception; his name is George. He lives alone and right across the street from us. It seems every time I go outside George is right there asking me what I'm doing. I don't know if he has ever been married but there is just something about him that I'm not too sure of. I try to avoid him if I can by going out the back door or through the garage."

"I guess the fact that we're all in the same age group leads to the friendliness of the Community."

"Well Maggie, it seems we both made the right choice."

"I guess so Joan. Now let me help you with the dinner. Joe is outside at the barbeque with Ian and I'm sure they both have a lot to say, they usually do."

"Ian told me Joe is having his hip surgery in a couple of weeks. We wish him a speedy recovery."

"Thank you Joan, I'll keep you informed of his progress."

"I'm sure he'll be up and around in no time," said Joan. "Joe is very healthy and strong."

"You're right, and thanks for the kind words. Now it's on with the salad."

Ian and Joe came into the kitchen with the barbequed steaks just as we were finishing setting the table. The salads and fruit were all prepared now so we sat down to a lovely meal.

Joan won the euchre game and the prize was a box of chocolates that I had provided. Someone had recently given me this box of chocolates but I was afraid to open it. I think I'm a chocoholic so if I open that box in no time it will be gone. Oh no! Ten pounds later I would regret every bite. I decided to share it. With four of us eating them it won't be quite so drastic.

"I'll share these chocolates with a cup of coffee before you have to leave."

"Thanks Joan. Could I help with the coffee?"

"Just get four mugs out of the third cupboard, thanks."

The next evening Joan calls and asks me if I would join her on a spy mission. I'm intrigued so, of course, I say yes. Ian said he was working late tonight and Joan wants to drive by his office to check for the car.

"Joan, I'll drive my car so you can be free to look around the parking lot."

"Okay Maggie, thanks."

There's no trace of Ian's car anywhere in this lot.

"Maggie, could you drive by the local restaurants and I'll look for the car there?"

"Sure Joan, but maybe Ian is on location as he is an architect."

"Could be but I don't think that's the case. After we check out the restaurants, maybe we should just go home."

"Joan, is that Ian's car in front of the hotel?"

"Yes it is, the bastard. Could we take a seat in the restaurant across the street and watch for him to come out?"

We take a seat at the window and just order coffee. It seems like we have been here for about an hour when Joan speaks up.

"Maggie, here comes Ian and he has a woman with him, holding onto his arm."

The two of them walk to a car that doesn't belong to Ian. They kiss and she gets into the car and drives away as Ian watches. Then Ian goes to his car and also leaves.

When Joan arrives home, Ian is already there.

"Where have you been? I've been here for hours worrying about you, Ian lied."

"Ian, I saw you coming out of the hotel with a floozy on your arm, so don't lie to me."

Ian apologizes profusely and says it will never happen again. The woman is someone who works at the office and they just got carried away. She is married too so neither of them want to get involved.

"Ian, I am very upset and disappointed in you. I never thought this could happen to us."

"Please forgive me Joan, and give me another chance. I promise it will never happen again."

"I will forgive you, Ian, but I will never forget. If you try this again I will leave you."

"Thank you, my Darling. I will never do this again. I'm so sorry I don't want to hurt you."

Chapter 7

The day of Joe's surgery finally arrived.

I followed Joe's stretcher as far as is permitted and then leaned over and gave him a kiss for good luck with the words, "I love you Joe."

Joe responded sleepily, as he had already been given some Demerol. "I love you too, my sweet Maggie." As they wheeled Joe through the doors to the operating room I could feel the tears well up in my eyes. Not wanting anyone to see me crying, I ducked quickly into a nearby washroom. I stayed in there for a few minutes collecting myself. I was nervous for Joe even though I kept telling him not to worry, everything would be fine. As I'm a worrywart I couldn't stop myself from thinking of all the things that could go wrong. The doctor told us general anesthetic always presents a risk but I tried to push that thought out of my mind as Joe had always been very healthy and there was no reason to think that he wouldn't do well.

I sat in the waiting room for what seemed forever before the doctor came out to talk to me. My heart skipped a beat (or two) when I saw Dr. Chalmers coming towards me.

"Your husband is going to recovery now and you can see him in about twenty minutes."

"Thank you Dr. Chalmers, I was so worried as Joe has never been in surgery before."

"You can relax now. Joe was a model patient; I only wish all my patients were so cooperative."

"Thanks again Doctor."

Finally, now, I feel I can breathe again. I think I'll go to the coffee shop down the hall and get a coffee and muffin. Now that I know Joe is okay I am starting to feel hungry. I couldn't even think about food while he was in surgery. My head is aching from the worry and not eating anything. I want to feel better before I go in to see Joe.

In twenty minutes, I was at Joe's side holding his hand as he started to regain consciousness after the anesthetic.

"Joe, I'm right here. Everything went well. How do you feel?"

I stayed for about another half an hour. I hated to leave him alone. Once Joe opened his eyes and recognized me, I felt happy enough to take the nurse's suggestion to go home and rest for a while.

That evening, I returned to the hospital. Joe was propped up on pillows and his face lit up when I walked into the room. I was thrilled to see him so happy and sitting up in bed.

"Hello Dear, how are you feeling?"

"Pretty good, I'm on pain medication. Thanks for coming."

"I saw you in recovery this morning," I said thinking he may not remember that I was there. He was very groggy and just recovering from the anesthetic.

"I don't remember that. I guess I was still asleep."

After a short visit I said, "I won't tire you today. I'll be back tomorrow; try to get some sleep." Joe looked a little beat. I know he would never say anything; he wouldn't want me to leave. So I took the initiative to force him to get some rest.

"Okay Honey, see you tomorrow."

I went home and answered a few phone calls from friends asking about Joe. I was pleased to tell them the operation had been successful.

The next afternoon and every subsequent one while Joe was in the hospital I visited him on my way home from work. On the second day there were three bouquets of flowers and Joan and Ian dropped by to check on Joe's progress.

On the day of Joe's discharge from hospital I was rushing around cooking and cleaning getting ready for his return. I was just taking a cake out of the oven when the telephone rang. It was Joe on the phone.

"Hi sweetheart, I have been signed out so could you please come and get me?"

"I can come right away. See you soon."

I arrived at the hospital about twenty minutes later and as I was passing the nurse's station on Joe's floor the head nurse stepped out of her office and asked me to join her for a minute. I went into her office and sat in the chair offered to me. I guess she is going to give me the list of instructions for Joe when I take him home. I know it will be difficult to keep Joe still for any length of time as he is a very energetic person.

Just as I sat down, Dr. Chalmers came in to join us. He was pale and looked anxious.

"Mrs. Henderson, I am very sorry but Joe developed a blood clot and when he got up it broke loose and travelled directly to his lung. Mrs. Henderson, he didn't suffer, he died instantly."

"No! I was just talking to him. You must be wrong." My head was reeling. I just spoke to him half an hour ago. My Joe, how could he be gone. I'm in disbelief, there must be a mistake. Joe can't be gone. I can't live without him. Oh! My head is pounding, I feel faint, what am I going to do now? I feel like I can hardly breathe. I want to die too.

"I'm very sorry. Would you like the nurse to take you to his room to see him?"

"Yes, I can't believe it."

"Mrs. Henderson, let me get you a drink of water and we'll sit here for a minute or two before we go to Joe's room," offered the nurse. She must know that my legs are like rubber. I don't think I can walk anywhere.

I'm crying and shaking so much that the nurse is hesitant to take me to Joe's room until she can calm me down a little.

"I want to see my Joe. Take me to Joe," I cried.

"I will as soon as I have a word with Dr. Chalmers." This is just a stall tactic, on the nurse's part, to give me a little more time. But they are just looking out for me as I'm very upset and I'm sure going to Joe's room will accelerate my condition.

When the nurse finally takes me to Joe's room, she stands back at the door to give me a chance to say goodbye. I know she is there but all I can see is my darling husband lying in the bed and not breathing. I can't believe what I'm seeing. I lean over and give him a kiss. He still feels warm. I tell him I love him. I'm crying so hard the sheets around Joe's shoulders are soaking wet. I stay as long as I can, not wanting to leave him. Finally the nurse says it's time to go. She ushers me from Joe's room. I'm still crying and very visibly shaken as she takes me back to her office.

"Who can I call for you, Mrs. Henderson? Do you have family I could call?"

"My three children please."

"I'll stay here with you until your family gets here. Would you like anything? Coffee maybe?"

"No thanks," I sobbed. How can I think about coffee or food when my whole life has just fallen apart? I don't think I will ever eat again.

Patricia drove me home after she and her brothers said goodbye to their father. James drove my car home and everyone followed.

Back at the house we all cried together from our devastating loss. "Mom, I'm going to stay here with you for a few days. James will bring my clothes tomorrow."

"Thank you Dear; I don't want to be alone tonight."

"Tomorrow we will make some phone calls and Peter and William will help me make the funeral arrangements," offered Patricia.

Chapter 8

A week after the funeral, Patricia and the boys are returning to work so Joan is taking a few days off work to stay with me. I'm still not able to function on my own. I don't care if I ever eat again. Every thought is about Joe. I can't concentrate on anything else. When someone talks to me I hear what they are saying but I couldn't care less. My world has just fallen apart and I have no will to continue. Everything I look at reminds me of Joe. I lie awake at night, crying and wondering why he had to leave me when we had so much more we wanted to do. I'll never do those things now without Joe. They will have no meaning. I just want to die. Please let me die too. My days and nights are just running together. I can't tell if it's day or night and what's worse, I don't care. I have never felt so much sorrow; I just can't describe the feeling of emptiness. My whole body shakes whenever I think about what is happening. My thoughts are interrupted:

"Maggie, can I do anything for you? Would you like to go out for lunch?"

"No thanks Joan, I just can't stop crying. I can't be with people right now. When I see a couple on television I burst out crying. I cry myself to sleep every night. I wake in the middle of the night crying and I just can't believe Joe is gone. I'm a real basket case."

"Maggie, what you're feeling is quite normal but I just wish there was something I could do to make you feel better. I hate to see you so lost and upset."

"Joan, you're helping me just by being here. Thanks for that. I know I just have to work through this myself." I don't see how I can ever get through such a tragedy. The kids phone a couple of times a day to check on me. I know they are upset too so I'm trying to be careful about what I say to them about my feelings; I don't want to have them worrying about me.

The next week, with Joan back at work, Sue called to invite me to join her and two other ladies for lunch.

"Thank you Sue, I'd like to get out of the house for a while." I think I should try to get back out in the world. I know it won't be easy but I do want to try. I hope I can hold it all together. I would hate to spoil things for the others. I know they are all my friends and trying to help but there's no way they could possibly understand the hell I'm in right now.

"I'll pick you up at twelve o'clock," Sue offered.

We arrived at the restaurant at twelve twenty. My three companions ordered wraps and coffee. I can't even be bothered to read the menu, nothing looks good to me anyway so I'll just ask for the same.

"How is your lunch Maggie?" asked Sue.

"Very good thanks and thanks for inviting me. I know I have to get out of the house and try to keep busy but I really don't feel much like it yet."

As I was talking, I looked up and caught a glimpse of a young couple holding hands. I think how wonderful this used to feel with Joe and know it will never happen again. I'm feeling very sorry for myself and upset that everyone has a significant other except me. I think the hardest thing for me right now, and probably the reason I don't like going out, is seeing couples together, holding hands, stealing a kiss or even just talking. I used to really enjoy every minute that Joe and I were together and seeing other couples just makes me feel completely lost. Will I ever return to some form of normalcy?

Why me? How did this happen to me? It's so unfair.

Sue noticed the tears in my eyes. I'm trying to blink them away but I guess it isn't working.

"Maggie, I'm going to a craft show tomorrow and it looks like fun. Would you like to join me?" I knew Sue was trying to distract me because she could see me watching people in the restaurant. Oh Sue! I appreciate your efforts but nothing is going to make me feel better. I feel like shit all the time. I have to come up with a polite response for my friend.

"Thank you Sue, I really appreciate all of your help. I'm not motivated to come up with anything myself."

"I know, that is what friends and neighbours are for. I'll pick you up at ten and if you wish we could also go for lunch."

"Thanks Sue, I'd love to go with you." I really had no desire to go anywhere, let alone to be with others but I know it is a necessary step to getting back to life.

After a couple of months, I went back to my job as a receptionist for a family physician. A long-time patient had booked an appointment that morning and when he arrived he had a lovely bouquet of flowers in his hand.

"Good morning Maggie, it's nice to have you back. The office wasn't the same without you. I hope these flowers will help to brighten your day," announced Stanley. It's nice of Stanley to say this but in my head and heart there is nothing that can help. I just feel like crying again but I have to hold it together now that I'm at work. I bite my tongue to try to distract myself from Stanley's kind words. Sometimes, for no apparent reason, I just burst out crying. I want to get back to life so I'm trying extra hard to control my feelings. Then someone like Stanley comes along and throws me for a loop.

"Thank you Stanley, I appreciate the gesture. Please take a seat and I will call you when the doctor is ready to see you."

"Thanks Maggie."

After Stanley's appointment with the doctor was over, and just as I expected, he stopped at my desk to talk.

"Maggie I would love to take you for dinner one evening if you would be interested."

I was quick to respond. I just got back to work following the death of my beloved husband and certainly was not looking for someone to replace him.

"Stanley, I thank you very much but I'm nowhere close to being ready to date at this time. I still miss Joe every minute of every day."

"I understand. When my wife died it was difficult for a long, long time afterwards. How about two friends going out for lunch?"

"Okay Stanley, but just as friends and absolutely nothing more."

Stanley agreed. After all, according to him, anything that got him closer to me was a step in the right direction. I know that Stanley has always liked me and enjoys talking to me whenever he's in the office. He usually overstays his appointment time to spend more time with me. Stanley even used to drop in during the day with a coffee or some candy for me even when he didn't have an appointment. He just said he was in the neighbourhood.

In a couple of days, I have a half day. Doctor Sinclair spends the afternoon in the hospital checking on his patients.

Stanley was there when I finished work, to pick me up for lunch.

We went to a small, quiet Italian Trattoria. Stanley had made a reservation for us.

"I hope you like Italian food Maggie. This restaurant is quiet and we can talk over lunch. The food here is excellent."

"Thank you Stanley. I love Italian cuisine."

"Have you been getting out much?" Stanley asked.

"I try to go to as many things as I can with the ladies group I belong to, but I don't date."

"I respect that but what about dinner next week as friends?"

I feel very uneasy at this point in time and I figure, typical man. He just thinks with his little head. Too bad he can't respect my feelings.

"I'm sorry Stanley but I told you I don't date and your offer sounds suspiciously like a date."

"I'm sorry if I offended you Maggie. I have admired you from afar for years now. I guess I'm just a little too anxious to get closer."

I immediately thought he is just anxious to get into my pants but this is not going to happen. I've had the very best in that department and I never want anyone else. Casual outings okay but nothing more and I'm adamant about this. I still hurt too much to even date for dinner. I feel like I'm cheating on Joe although I'm sure he would want me to be happy. Right now I'm happy just doing my own thing. I'm not looking for a replacement for my Joe.

After lunch, I went directly home not wanting to linger any longer with Stanley who obviously had an ulterior motive.

Next time Stanley asks me out, and I know there will be a next time; I'm not going to accept. Why should I put myself in an uncomfortable position? It's obvious that we are not looking for the same thing. I think when a man loses his wife he is in a hurry to replace her and have someone looking after him again. Women are very different; our feelings for our mate run very deep. Women seem to be able to manage very well on their own. At this time I hate being alone but I think I feel even worse at the thought of another man. So, I guess I will be living alone for the rest of my life. I can't see me with anyone but Joe; he was my other half and now he's gone. Just the thought of Joe makes the tears well up in my eyes again. At least I'm in my own kitchen now, I'm thinking as the tears stream down my cheeks. Will this empty feeling ever go away? Now I must pull myself together and stop crying or my face will be all swollen and my eyes will be red and, of course, that is the time someone will come to the door.

Chapter 9

A few days later, as I was going out my front door to meet Sue, I heard George, who lives across the street. George was calling:

"Maggie how are you?"

"Just fine George, thank you."

I let my mind wander to the past few weeks. I feel that there have been a few rather strange things happening with George but one at a time they don't seem too bad. Now that I add them all together I wonder just what he is up to?

Every time I go outside George is right there. Does he just sit at the window waiting for me to come outside? There's something rather creepy about George's actions. I'm glad I decided to use the back door or even go through the garage. I feel uneasy whenever he's around. I can't pinpoint the reason. Maybe it's just my being suspicious now that I don't have Joe to protect me. I always felt so safe when he was with me but I will be extra careful where George is concerned.

Later that week I was in the kitchen making some tomato soup for my lunch when there was a knock on my door. When I answered it, I was surprised to see George with a handful of flowers. What on earth is he up to now? Not wanting to be rude, in case this was just a friendly gesture, I accepted the flowers.

"Maggie I brought you some flowers from my garden. I was weeding today and I thought how nice it would be to share some flowers with you."

"Thank you George but please don't give me any more gifts. I feel uncomfortable accepting them." I feel really uncomfortable with anything that George does. I am newly single and not aware of what to expect from men. I am very afraid of insulting someone but even more afraid to lead them on.

"Well Maggie, I was hoping you might join me for the dance in the Community Centre this Saturday?"

"Sorry George. I don't go to dances anymore," I said very nervously. I was hoping that he would accept it and just leave. George really scares me. He seems to have a funny idea about life. I don't think he has ever been married and I have never seen him with a woman. I'm going to keep my distance from him. He really is strange.

"Maggie, I have watched you for some time now and you appear very lonely. Let me help with that." As if going out with George would help me. It's sure to make things worse, the man freaks me out.

"No thanks George and please leave me alone. I'm doing just fine."

After that encounter with George, I did use the back door and I cut across the backyard to Sue or Barb's houses.

On Saturday, Joan and Ian invited me to go to the market with them. Since I had already told my friend about my creepy neighbour, Joan came to my door to meet me and walk me to the car. I feel so silly having a bodyguard to go out of my own house but I really don't trust George.

"Joan, I love this market. Usually I buy lots of vegetables and fruits for preserving."

"How about you and I making Chili sauce together this year?" suggested Joan.

"I have an excellent recipe for Granny's Chili Sauce and we can make it at my house." I have all the pots, jars and utensils needed. I've always done sauces, jams and jellies but this year, with Joe gone, I don't have the desire or the will to make them. Since Joan is asking me, and I know she's aware that I always do this at the end of summer, I feel I should accept. Joan is trying very hard to help me through this difficult time and I do appreciate it.

"How about next weekend?"

"Perfect I'll come over at nine a.m."

"Okay then let's buy what we need here at the market today."

Ian carried all the vegetables and fruit to the car and when we arrived at my house he put everything in the garage. The back of the garage is very cool as there are no windows to let in the sun. I have an old fridge in there so if it gets hot I can move some of the fruit to the fridge. I'll try to avoid this as fresh, warm fruit and vegetables are best.

Next Saturday Joan arrived at nine a.m.

"Come in dear friend," I called from the kitchen.

"I'm here to make the Chili; hope you are in the mood."

"Joan I'm glad you're here. I need a friend today."

"What's wrong Maggie?"

"I couldn't sleep last night. I miss having a man's arms around me. Even more than that, and I feel guilty, I miss the intimacy. What can I do to relieve these terrible feelings?"

"When Ian was sick a few years ago I bought a personal vibrator. It really helped me. I know you're not ready for another man and you don't want to jump into bed with just anyone. I think if you take care of yourself as I did you'll be fine."

"Thanks Joan but I feel disgusting even considering such a thing."

"Maggie it's a normal, healthy part of life and it could prevent you from making a big mistake."

"Enough! Let's get on with the Chili."

"This is the first time I have made Chili, so please tell me what to do," confessed Joan.

"It's very easy and I'll guide you through it."

The Chili was a success. We ended up with twelve bottles each. That should last me a long time since now I only cook for one.

On Wednesday evening, with nothing on television, I sat curled up by the fire with a good book in my hands. All of a sudden, there were lights flashing in the living room window. I jumped up and ran to the window as a fire truck stopped in front of Gordon's house. Very soon after that the ambulance arrived. Someone had called 911. In this adult community, emergency vehicles turn their sirens off at the gate so I didn't hear them coming. I grabbed a jacket and ran outside to join the growing number of concerned neighbours. In about fifteen minutes, the ambulance pulled out of the driveway with Gordon on board. The fire engine had already left. George came over to me and put his arm around my shoulders to comfort me, so he said. I knew what he really wanted and I pulled away quickly moving over to stand beside Sue.

As the neighbours stood talking and wishing Gordon well, Matt emerged from Gordon's house. He was visibly shaken and he looked very upset. Matt walked slowly towards the waiting crowd. As he choked on his words he announced that Gordon had passed away. He had had a massive heart attack.

Gordon and Matt had been friends for a few years now and Matt had just gone over to check on his friend as he did every evening. Matt found Gordon clutching his chest. His breathing was laboured and he was pale and sweaty. Matt immediately called 911 and then put Gordon into a sitting position to make it easier for him to breathe. As the paramedics were working on Gordon, he succumbed to his illness.

I felt so guilty for what I was thinking at this particular time.

Matt looks so upset all I want to do is run up to him and wrap my arms around him to comfort him. Where are these feeling coming from? I hardly know this man. I really can't do what I would like to do. I find Matt so very attractive and exciting. Maybe I'm feeling this way because it's so soon after I lost Joe and I know what Matt must be feeling, losing his best friend.

The crowd is starting to disburse so I think I will go home and comfort myself with a glass of wine and maybe a couple of chocolates. My vibrator sits unused in my bottom drawer. Maybe this would be a good time to bring it out. Matt has unknowingly left me feeling raw and lonely.

Over the next few months I was able to keep myself very busy. I found when I was busy I had less time to think about Joe. He was always on my mind, day and night, but further to the back when I was busy. I keep myself very busy with lots of meetings as I have joined the boards of two activity groups in the Community.

"Next Sunday I'm having a cookie exchange at my house," said Sue. "If you would like to come, make six dozen cookies and you can choose six dozen cookies made by the other ladies, so you will have a nice assortment."

"I can make rum balls. Would that be okay?"

"Perfect Maggie, I'm glad you're coming."

Once again as I went out the front door to go to Sue's house, George was standing in his driveway across the street. Of course, he spotted me as I was walking to Sue's.

"May I help you carry something?" George begged.

"No thanks George, I'm doing fine."

I increased my stride in order to get away from George. As I arrived at Sue's I was out of breath. When Sue questioned me I told her about George.

"I've always had a funny feeling around George," said Sue. "If he continues to creep you out, you could get a restraining order to keep him away."

"I know I've thought of it but I don't want to make bad relations with my neighbours. After all, we do have to live here."

"Just be careful Maggie and don't let your guard down when he's around. I'm not sure that he wouldn't use this time to take advantage of you."

When the fun of the cookie exchange was over, Sue walked me home and as expected, George was sitting on his porch just watching.

"Lock your doors and windows when I leave," instructed Sue.

"I will and thanks for walking me home." Again, I feel foolish having my friends walk me home in my own neighbourhood.

"Call me, Maggie, if George bothers you tonight."

I was frightened but even through my fear I was thinking about Matt.

The night was uneventful.

Thank goodness, George didn't come around after he saw Sue. I'm glad I have such good friends. At this time, without Joe, I really need all the support I can get.

Chapter 10

As I open my eyes this morning I can see it is a bright, beautiful day. My thoughts are always on Joe first thing in the morning and last thing at night. I can almost feel him here in bed beside me. Oh! How I wish that were true. I miss him so much. Now I know what people mean when they say "I miss him so much it hurts." He's on my mind every waking hour and as I think about us, the tears are coming into my eyes. I'll get up now and try to make myself feel better, although I can't imagine how. I feel as if half of me has been torn apart and it stings. Sometimes a shower helps, so in I go. This is a day off work for me as Dr. Sinclair is out of town, so I'm going out this morning. I'm going for coffee over at the Activities Centre with Sue and Barb. The men don't usually go for coffee. It seems a little feminine an activity for them. I have been very lucky to have girlfriends to go out with.

As I was putting on a necklace, to match the green sweater I was wearing, the phone rang. I picked it up in the bedroom.

"Hello."

"Hi Maggie, this is George. Are you going for coffee this morning?"

"As a matter of fact, yes, I am."

"I would love to go with you."

"Sorry George, I am going with the ladies."

"I will see you there then and maybe I can sit with you."

"George, I have asked you politely not to bother me and now I must insist that you leave me alone."

George did show up for coffee but he didn't try to sit with us.

"Sure hope he got the message this time," I remarked to Sue.

After the coffee, Barb, Sue and I went shopping for dresses to wear to the Christmas party at the Community banquet room. The party was going to consist of a turkey dinner followed by a play put on by some of the residents. Following that, the singing of Christmas Carols and then a dance. I was planning to leave after the singing and before the dancing started. Joe and I used to love to dance but I have no desire to dance with anyone else. I may never dance again. A dance is not fun for a widowed lady. Most people are in couples and, believe it or not, wives don't want their husbands dancing with a widow. Maybe they think we want to steal them. This is certainly not the case for most of us. We just want to have a little fun. It's difficult being a widow. Your married friends don't invite you over as often as they did when you were a couple. Singles parties are not the answer as most of us are not looking to replace our husbands. I will never sit alone in a bar. This is just inviting trouble, in my opinion, and one night stands don't appeal to me.

Sue bought a red knit dress that hugged her perfect figure very nicely. Barb picked a lovely blue dress which was sheered at the waist to hide a few extra pounds that she had gained recently. I found a plain black dress. It has a V-neck and sports a patent leather belt. It seems appropriate to me that I wear black.

On the day of the party, I spent the afternoon at my favourite spa. I had a mani pedi and my hairdresser put my hair up in curls. She told me I really am a strikingly beautiful woman but I don't care. There's no one I'm out to impress.

Barb and Sam just arrived to pick me up. Sue and Jack are already in the car. The five of us are going to sit together for dinner and the evening's events. These are my very dear friends but I feel like a fifth wheel with no partner. As I look around, it seems everyone has a significant other except me. I always notice people holding hands or just talking and it makes me feel so lonely. Maybe it was a mistake to come to this party tonight. I don't see how I could possibly enjoy it alone.

The dinner was delicious but when the carolling was over, Sam offered to drive me home as he knew I didn't want to stay for the dance.

Sam dropped me at my door and sat in the car until I was safely inside. Then he returned to the dance to join the others.

I was tired as this was really the first evening party since Joe died. It took a lot out of me both physically and mentally.

I decided to get ready for bed and to sit by the fire with my book for a while to settle down before going to bed.

I went to the kitchen and poured myself a glass of my favourite red wine, grabbed my book off the table and proceeded to the living room to turn on the electric fireplace.

About half an hour later as I was just starting to feel quite mellow, the effect of the wine I figure, I thought I heard someone on the front porch. I got up to look outside but saw nothing. Returning to my book and starting to relax again, there was a tapping sound at my back door. This scared me and I jumped up to check but this time I took a knife out of the kitchen drawer. I'm not sure what I was planning to do with a kitchen knife but nevertheless I took it with me. I was quite frightened and tip-toed to the door. I cautiously moved the curtain a very tiny bit to see out. Again there was nothing there. I know that I hadn't been imagining it and I didn't know what to do. My best friends were at the dance and I was hesitant to call the police in case it was just the wind or something simple. As I return to the living room I could hear another noise that sounds suspiciously like someone trying to pry a window open. Through the sheers that I have on the front windows I could see the outline of a man and I immediately recognized George. What am I going to do? My palms are sweating, my head is whirling and I suddenly feel sick to my stomach. Oh! How I hate living alone.

What is he trying to do; break and enter?

I'm so frightened as I'm running to my bedroom to call the police. Someone is banging on my front door. My heart is in my mouth.

"What do I do now? Certainly not answer the door to that crazed George."

"Maggie, Maggie it's Barb and Sam. Are you okay? We just noticed your front window is open and we know you locked them."

I breathed a sigh of relief as I ran to the door. When I related the evening's events, Barb told me to pack an overnight bag and go home with them. Sam said he would contact the police. As soon as Sam drove up, George ran off so nobody saw him except me. But through the curtains, I am certain that it was George.

Chapter 11

Today is Sunday and normally I would try to sleep in but I'm not at home. Barb and Sam have been good to me, taking care of me last night and offering to call the police. I'm not sure if Sam has called them yet but I'm just heading downstairs for breakfast so I'll ask him. As I reach the kitchen door, I see Barb making pancakes.

"Good morning Barb."

"Good morning, did you sleep well?"

"The bed was comfortable, thanks, but I have so much on my mind that I very seldom get a full night's sleep."

I didn't want to make her feel badly by telling her my mind is always full of thoughts of Joe so I just said my concerns were about George. This is true but not the whole story. Being with Barb and Sam and seeing how happy they are together just makes me feel worse. I can't wait until breakfast is over and I can return to my own house.

"Good morning, ladies." Sam arrived in the kitchen just as the pancakes were ready.

"Coffee anyone?"

"Yes, thank you Barb."

"I called the police last night Maggie and they are coming over here at ten o'clock."

"Thanks Sam, that gives us about three quarters of an hour for breakfast."

The police arrived on time and we all sat in the family room. I'm very nervous. The only thing I have to go on are my feelings. I would hate to accuse an innocent man. Maybe I just want it to be George because I feel a little funny around him. Not that he has ever done anything to cause this distrust.

The police have a lot of questions and I'm trying to answer them to the best of my ability and as honestly as possible.

"Now we have all the information we need to check this out. We'll get back to you as soon as possible. In the meantime, please be extra careful and call us if you notice anything."

"Could you post a guard at Maggie's house tonight just in case he tries anything?" Sam had a very good suggestion.

"We could send someone over from eleven to seven. He'll sit in a driveway just down the street as we know those people are in Florida right now."

"Thank you," said Sam.

The police left and I got up to leave as well.

"Maggie, please stay. I don't like the thought of your being alone in your house."

"I'll be fine. I have laundry to do before I go to work tomorrow."

"Okay but phone me two or three times so I know you're alright."

"I will and thanks for all your help."

Back at home, I started to sort the laundry. Why isn't Joe here? I really need him now. The tears started again. I guess it is all this stress and not having Joe to help me. I must pull myself together and carry on. I'll call Barb at lunchtime.

As I was folding the first load of clothes, the phone rang.

"Hello," I said very cautiously hoping it wasn't George.

"How are you?" It was Sue. Barb has been talking to her and Sue just wants to help.

"I'm fine thanks, just doing some laundry."

"I just made a nice big salad and a lemon cake. Jack is out visiting his uncle in the hospital so I thought I would come to your house and we could eat lunch together."

"Thanks that would be great. I'll put on the coffee." I know Barb has told Sue that I shouldn't be alone. I'm thankful because I don't want to be alone. Very few people choose to live alone but circumstances cause them to. I hate being alone, so Sue's invitation for lunch is very welcome.

As we sat enjoying our lemon cake, the phone rang.

"Hello."

"Hello Mrs. Henderson, this is Detective Farley. Would it be convenient for my partner and me to come over in about half an hour? We have some news about George for you."

"Of course, see you soon."

"Sue, the police are coming over with news about George. Would you like to stay? I think I should call Barb and Sam as well."

"Good idea Maggie and yes I'm very interested."

Barb and Sam came right over and the police arrived shortly after.

When the doorbell rang I practically ran to answer it.

"Good afternoon Mrs. Henderson. I'm Detective Farley and this is my partner Detective Becker."

"Please come in. I've asked my neighbours to join us. I hope that's okay?"

"Certainly, this concerns them as well."

Detective Farley spoke first.

"You can rest assured George Bingham has been arrested and is in custody as we speak."

I breathed a huge sigh of relief, so much that everyone laughed.

"Mr. Bingham has been arrested in three other provinces for stalking and annoying ladies. He is currently wanted for the abduction of a young woman in Edmonton. Mr. Bingham changed his name: he is actually George Kowalski. The Alberta police have had a warrant out for his arrest for five years. Mr. Kowalski will be transferred to Alberta and he will be in prison for quite some time."

"I'm so happy that now I will be able to sleep without worrying."

"Thank you Mrs. Henderson for trusting your feelings and reporting him to the police. You have helped to catch a wanted man."

After everyone left, I went back to doing my laundry but this time I don't have to look over my shoulder every time I hear a noise.

One week later I heard a tapping sound outside. It's the middle of the day and I know George is in prison so I will just look out the door. Well, glory be! There's a "For Sale" sign on George's lawn. Now I don't need to worry about him ever coming back.

Chapter 12

Well it's Monday morning and time to go to work. At least I don't have to sneak out the back door anymore. It's been a very exciting weekend with the dinner/dance, George's antics and then the police and George's arrest.

As I pull into the parking lot at work I see a car that I recognise but it takes me a minute to figure out why. Oh no! It's Stanley. I sure hope he's here for an appointment with the doctor and not to bother me again. I've had such an eventful weekend and I'm not in the mood for Stanley. I have to get out of the car and open the office. The doctor should be here in about five or ten minutes. Why is Stanley here so early? I feel a little nervous. My feelings were right on with George. I'm not afraid of Stanley; I just don't like the attention he gives me. I'm not interested in dating him but I know he still wants me. Well Maggie, stay strong.

I unlock the door and start turning on the lights when I hear the door open. I hope it's the doctor but I fear it's Stanley. I have to prepare the rooms to receive patients in half an hour so I busy myself with this task and ignore the front office for now. I am feeling very shaky; if it was the doctor he would have said good morning by now. My fears become a reality when I walk slowly towards the front of the office. I look into the reception area and there sits Stanley. As soon as I enter his sight line he jumps to his feet and walks to my desk.

"Good morning Stanley. Do you have an appointment?"

"No Maggie. I came in to see you. I can't get you off my mind and I wondered if you would be willing to give me a second chance and possibly join me for lunch?"

I know I must stay strong but it's a difficult thing for me to intentionally hurt someone.

"Thank you Stanley, I do appreciate the offer but as I told you before I'm not ready to date. I know going to lunch is not a real date but I'm afraid that is what it would lead to. Thank you again but I'm sorry I have to refuse."

"I'm sorry too, Maggie. I will give you a little more time and then maybe you would reconsider?"

I can't see myself ever going out with Stanley. He's just not my type even if I was willing to date. He's too pushy for me; I can't imagine being married to someone like that. I like an equal partnership just the way Joe and I were. It was a perfect marriage and he would be impossible to replace. So I'm not dating or even looking.

"Sorry Stanley."

Later today I have an appointment with my own physician. I haven't seen her since Joe died. I hope everything is okay. I am normally very healthy and I don't have any complaints. This appointment is just for a physical examination.

I arrive at the doctor's office at four fifteen as scheduled. I'm taken right in and the doctor and her assistant come in for my examination. After she checks my eyes, ears, blood pressure and pulse she asks me to undress for my pap smear. I hate this test but I guess it's necessary even though I'm no longer sexually active.

Once I'm dressed and the exam is over, the doctor enters the room again.

"Everything looks good, Maggie, except your blood pressure is a little high 140/98."

"I've had a very difficult weekend." I explain the situation with my neighbour.

"That certainly could contribute to the blood pressure rise. I think rather than starting you on medication we can try a more conservative approach. I know you are careful with your diet so why don't we add some more exercise to your daily regime. How about a half an hour walk each night after dinner. Could you manage that?"

"Yes I don't see why not. I'll start this evening."

"Okay Maggie and I would like to see you again in two weeks to check your progress. Try to relax a little more. Make an appointment with the receptionist on your way out and good luck with everything. I know things are difficult for you right now."

"Thank you doctor."

I think I'll pick up a veggie wrap on the way home so I don't have to cook. It's getting late and I want to start walking tonight. I've never had a problem with my blood pressure before so it must be all the stress. Guess I have to work harder at taking care of myself.

Chapter 13

I just got home from work and I'm changing into my sweats for walking. I think I'll have pasta and a salad for dinner tonight. I'm hungry and since I have nothing prepared, I'll just cook some fusilli with pesto. After dinner I can go out for my walk. I'm feeling much better with all the walking I've been doing. It's almost two weeks now and I'll have to report back to my doctor in a couple of days. I'm feeling better so I hope my blood pressure is at a better level.

The pasta and salad were delicious and now I'm ready for my walk. It's a little cool outside tonight so I think I should wear a light jacket over my sweat top.

I think I'll walk to the Community Centre and hopefully see someone I can talk to for a few minutes. It's very lonely always doing everything by myself. I miss Joe's company every day. Oh, there are a few people here but they seem to be in couples. Everyone seems to be in couples these days. I guess they are going inside to play cards. I can't sit and play cards because I have to continue walking. As I round the corner to the next street all I see is someone walking a dog. Another street with no one outside. I guess I will head back towards home. I've been out for almost an hour. I can see a man further down my street but I don't recognize him from here. I'm sure I'm safe especially since George is no longer here. I'll just walk swiftly and keep going. As I get a little closer I can see that it's Matt. He's out walking too.

"Hi Matt, how are you tonight?"

"I'm fine, thanks Maggie. How are you?"

"I'm good too. It's nice to see you."

"Walk with me for a while Maggie?"

I know I was heading home but this opportunity may not come again and I really would like to get to know Matt a little better. I don't know why but getting to know him somehow seems important. I'm not looking for a boyfriend but maybe just a friend.

"Okay I would love to."

As we walked around the block Matt told me that he walks often because sitting alone makes him feel sad. I know exactly what he means because I feel the same way.

"Maggie, I know you are not dating and neither am I but would you be open to joining me one day for lunch?"

"I'd like that very much Matt and thanks. Check your calendar and I'll check mine. I think the weekend would be best as through the week I usually only take an hour for lunch."

"Thanks Maggie, I'll call you when we get back home tonight."

"Okay I look forward to your call."

I'm glad our walk is over because now I'm rushing home to wait for Matt's call. I don't know what is going on with me. I do find him very attractive but I'm still in love with Joe and I think I always will be. I would certainly welcome a good friend.

The next afternoon I'm on my way home and I spot Ian's car again. I think I'll follow him and see what is going on. I'm far enough behind Ian's car so as not to be recognized and he pulls up to an office building and I park across the street and watch. I don't recognize the building but as I sit there a strange woman appears in the doorway. Ian jumps out of his car and walks over to greet her. They kiss and proceed to Ian's car. It looks like he might be giving this woman a ride home so I decide to follow them. Maybe I can get more information for Joan. We drive for about twenty minutes and then Ian pulls up in front of a small bungalow in the suburbs. The woman gets out of the car but not before she and Ian hug and kiss a few times. I write down the address and proceed on home undetected.

The next morning, I call the office that we were at yesterday.

"Hello," I said when someone answered. I was being careful not to give my name.

"This may sound confusing to you but I'm looking for a good architect and I know one of your employees is dating the person I would like to hire. But I have forgotten her name."

"Oh, you mean Carol."

"Yes, that's her. What is her last name again?"

"Pearson. Could I have her call you?"

"No thanks but if you could give me her number I'll call her tonight after work."

This poor unsuspecting receptionist supplies the number and I have all I need. Boy! I'm really a super sleuth.

This evening I'll invite Joan over to my house and fill her in with the details. I hate to hurt my friend this way but she deserves to know.

The next day Joan leaves Ian and applies for a legal separation.

Chapter 14

When I go into work this morning, I am going to hand in my resignation. This won't be easy as I've worked for the same doctor for eleven years. Now that I'm sixty-three, I feel like cutting back to part time work to give myself more time for the activities I enjoy. With the pension I now get from Joe I feel I can afford to cut back a little.

"Good morning, Dr. John." I call him Dr. John but his name is actually Dr. John Sinclair.

"Morning and how are you Maggie?"

"I'm well thank you but when you have a minute I'd like to have a word with you."

"Sure Maggie, just let me get my coat off and then come into my office."

I'm shaking, this doctor is so good to me and I hate to leave. I'll offer to train someone new. Maybe that will take some of the sting out of my leaving.

I knock on Dr. John's door and I hear:

"Come in Maggie and take a seat. What's on your mind this morning?"

"Well, doctor I feel terrible doing this because I really enjoy working for you but I'm handing in my resignation. I would just like part time work now."

"Maggie I'm so sorry. You've been such a huge help to me. However, I do understand. What are your plans? When do you want to leave?"

"I have no definite plans and I would certainly stay until I've trained my replacement."

"I appreciate your consideration and I'll start looking for someone immediately," Dr. John remarked. "Maggie, if you know of anyone who may be interested please send her in. How about offering the position to Barbara, the young lady who filled in for your bereavement leave?"

"I know Barbara did an excellent job for you, but she has just accepted a full time position in the business office at the hospital. I'll do my best to find someone as soon as possible."

I went out to my desk fighting back tears. I do enjoy working for Dr. John and I can't picture my life not seeing him anymore. I'll busy myself with pulling charts for tomorrow's patients then maybe I can forget what I just did. The first patient of the day just came in the door so now I, at least, have someone to talk to. I'm taking our first patient into room #3 when the front door opens and there stands Stanley. I quickly look at the appointments on the computer and thankfully see that he is our second patient. I was afraid he might be here to ask for another date. I don't need that today.

"Good morning, Stanley. The doctor will be with you shortly."

"Thanks Maggie and how are you?"

"Just fine thank you," I said and quickly turned to my computer to look busy.

When I took Stanley into room #2 and I prepared the room for the doctor's procedure, he put his hand on my shoulder and told me how much he misses me. I said, "I'm sorry" and quickly left the room.

When Stanley's appointment was over he winked at me as he passed my desk. Then thankfully he left the office.

We are busy this morning with several more patients but now the last lady is leaving. I think I'll stay in my office for a quiet lunch today. I have some yogurt and fruit in the fridge.

The phone rings and Dr. John is on the other end.

"Maggie, could you please come into my office for a minute before you go for lunch?"

"I'll be right in doctor."

When I enter his office he signals for me to sit. I'm a bit nervous. What could he possibly want?

"Maggie, I have been thinking, I really hate to lose you. What if I hire a part time person and you could stay on as the other part time person?"

"Sort of like job sharing?" I asked.

"Yes I guess you could say that. You could train the new person before you switch to part time and then you could work alternate days."

"I think that would be great. Then I wouldn't have to leave completely." This arrangement could work and I feel wonderful about not leaving. Boy! This man is good to me.

After two weeks of interviews, we are choosing Gail. She seems to suit this office the best of all the people we interviewed. Dr. John and I interviewed together as he felt I would know better who would fit our needs. I really appreciate his confidence in me.

Gail is in her late thirties and the mother of two teenagers. She is looking to re-enter the work force and she feels this would be the perfect fit for her.

"Gail, welcome to our office. I hope you enjoy working for Dr. John as much as I do. He is more than fair and very polite with staff and patients alike. As you know this is a part-time position but can you work full time for two weeks and I will work with you to help you learn the procedures of this office. After your training we can alternate days. If you would like three days a week I could take the other two."

"Thank you for this opportunity. I will happily work full time for the next two weeks. When we alternate, which days would you like me to work?"

"How about Monday, Wednesday and Friday? I'll take Tuesday and Thursday. This isn't set in stone so if you need to switch a day sometimes, I could fill in for you. Could you start next Monday for training?"

"That sounds perfect, thanks Maggie."

"You're welcome. Now that we have arranged the hours would you please go to Dr. John's office and he'll discuss your salary and benefits."

"See you Monday, Gail called out as she left the office."

Just then the phone rang.

"Good morning, Dr. Sinclair's office. How may I help you?"

A very friendly voice on the other end of the line said: "You could accept my invitation for lunch tomorrow."

My heart skipped a beat. It's Matt. Why do I feel this way every time I hear his voice? I'm still in love with Joe. Take a chance Maggie! I am so frightened to go out with another man. It has always been Joe for me and I was so comfortable with him. Now I guess I have to take a step out of my comfort zone, but I just want a friend, nothing more.

"I would love to have lunch with you tomorrow. Dr. John is at the hospital tomorrow afternoon so I could take the time off."

"I'll pick you up at your office. Is twelve thirty okay?"

"Yes, I look forward to having lunch with you."

"Me too Maggie."

My heart is doing flip flops as I hang up the phone. This man is so considerate and he is not out to jump my bones as I suspect Stanley is. What should I wear? I want something nice but conservative and not too sexy. I have a nice blue and white dress that would work under my lab coat for the morning's work and then with a necklace for lunch.

Chapter 15

I'm just finishing up with our morning patients and it's twelve fifteen.

My stomach is starting to jump around. I'm so nervous. I know this is not a date but it feels very much like one. What would Joe think of this luncheon? I'm sure he would tell me to go and enjoy myself. I'll go but I'm not sure if I'll enjoy it with someone other than Joe.

At exactly twelve thirty, Matt pulls up in his grey Lexus. My shaky legs are carrying me to the front door of the office and then to the door of the Lexus which is being held open by my lunch partner, Matt.

"Good afternoon Maggie. I hope you're hungry."

"Hi Matt. Where are we going?"

"I've chosen a small French Bistro where we can sit and talk quietly. I hope you like this type of food."

"Yes, I enjoy most cuisines."

As we enter the restaurant the hostess greets us.

"Good afternoon Mr. Stafford."

Since Matt had made a reservation, she escorts us to our table in the corner, by the window. This is perfect but looks suspiciously like a romantic area. I hope Matt is not trying to fool me with a lunch invitation. Have I read the signs wrong? Matt please *don't* disappoint me.

"I hope this table is to your liking Maggie. If it isn't we can switch."

"This is fine Matt."

"Would you like a glass of wine?"

"No thank you, I'll just have water with no lemon please."

I like wine with a meal but I'm afraid to lower my resistance to this gorgeous man. I want to be in full control the whole lunch time. Wine sometimes makes me a little careless and I can't afford that feeling today.

We both ordered crepes and a small side salad.

"While we're waiting for our lunch, Matt said: "Why don't you tell me a little about yourself Maggie?"

"Well there really isn't too much to tell. You already know all about Joe. He was the love of my life and the father of my children."

"How many children do you have?"

"Three, my daughter, Patricia is married to James a paediatrician and they have given me two lovely grandchildren. I have two sons Peter and William who are both still single." All my children live fairly close, so they visit me often."

"Now Matt, it's your turn. I know nothing about you."

"Well Maggie, I was married to a wonderful woman for twenty five years. She suffered from cancer for several years but succumbed to it a few years ago. I still miss her."

"Do you have any children?"

"Just one son, Brian, but he lives out west and only visits twice a year. I go to visit him usually twice a year as well."

We talked a lot as we ate our lunch. Matt is a very good conversationalist and I do enjoy listening to him. He can talk about almost anything and he is quite knowledgeable as well. I told him a few stories about life with my children and, of course, Joe. I felt comfortable sharing these memories with Matt as he knew Joe. Matt talked about his late wife and his son and I could tell he was a family man and enjoyed married life. I could feel that Matt was very much in love with his wife and this made me feel more comfortable as we were becoming friends. I feel good sitting and talking with Matt but there is just something that I can't put my finger on. I'm not sure what I'm feeling but I know there is more.

After coffee we drove back home.

"Maggie, I thoroughly enjoyed our lunch today. I respect the fact that you are not dating but would you like to accompany me, as a friend, to dinner and Cirque du Soleil? I just got two free tickets for next Friday evening and I hate going out alone."

"Thank you Matt, that would be very nice."

The rest of the week is going by very slowly as all I can think about is Friday evening with Matt. I shouldn't be this excited to go out with him when I still love and miss Joe so much.

I have to choose my wardrobe; something nice enough for dinner and a show but not too fancy. I don't know how Matt is feeling and I don't want to lead him on. Black is always appropriate for dinner so I will wear my black pant suit and a pale pink silk blouse. That won't be too sexy. I will make an appointment to get my hair cut and curled on Thursday after work. As I'm still on full days I have to go at night. I don't like thinking about Matt this much. I feel like I am betraying Joe. How can I stop? If this goes on too long I think I'll break it off, whatever *it* is, with Matt. I don't like feeling so confused and upset.

Friday is finally here and Matt is at my door.

"Good evening Maggie, you look lovely."

I could see Matt's eyes going from top to bottom as he checked out his "date" or should I say friend.

"Good evening to you as well, Matt."

Matt looked fabulous in black pants, a sports jacket and turtle neck. I'm excited to be seen on the arm of such a good looking man.

"I've made a reservation downtown for dinner so we can be close to the theatre. This way we can enjoy our dinner and not have to worry about traffic problems on the way to the show."

"What a wonderful idea Matt. You've planned this out quite well."

"I just hope you have a good time Maggie. You deserve to be happy and you've gone through a lot lately."

I have to look away. I hope Matt can't see the tears in my eyes. When anyone sympathizes with my plight, I start to feel a little upset and, of course, those telltale tears start again. Blink Maggie blink. This usually clears my eyes so I can face my friend and continue our conversation.

"I'm sure it will be lovely."

The dinner and the show were very enjoyable. Cirque du Soleil was terrific. I've never seen this show before although I know it has been around for several years. Actually I don't go to shows anymore. Without Joe, I'd have to go alone and that's not going to happen.

On our drive home, Matt started saying how much he enjoyed my company.

"I'm flattered Matt, thank you for this wonderful evening."

"If you feel up for it, I would like to take you out again."

"I think that would be very nice."

"It's a date then. Oops! Sorry, just friends. Okay?"

"Yes okay."

"I'll walk you to your door Maggie."

Walking up the front walk Matt took my hand. I feel a tingle at his touch. Oh boy! I think I might be in trouble. I shouldn't be having these feelings for any man. Matt has always given me butterflies even when we first met at Barb and Sam's party. I wanted to set him up with one of my girlfriends as Joe was still alive then. Now Matt seems interested in me. He leans in for a good night kiss and I turn my cheek. Matt seems happy with this and does the double kiss, once on each cheek. This works for me right now.

As I'm getting ready for bed I can't stop thinking how polite and nice Matt is. Not to forget drop dead gorgeous; please excuse the pun. I know Joe would say go for it, be happy but I feel guilty looking at another man in this way. When I get into bed the tears start again. What to do. I still miss Joe. How can I have true feelings for Matt? I'm falling asleep with two beautiful men on my mind. How lucky can one woman be? Hope I feel better in the morning.

Chapter 16

As I'm enjoying the first coffee of the day and a piece of toast with honey, I can hear some noises out on the street.

Looking out the living room window I can see there is a moving truck across the road. Someone is moving into George's house. Hope the new people are not as crazy as the last person.

I think I'll sit by the window, with my coffee, and see who's moving in. Hey! They have a dog. There's a fairly large crate in the driveway and a beautiful golden lab in it. I love dogs and cats, for that matter. Now if I wait a little longer maybe I will see my new neighbours. A widow would be okay but I hope it's not another single man. In this community we get a lot of widows and widowers because of the fifty-five plus stipulation. Oh wait a minute; I see the front door opening. Oh oh, it is a man. He looks in his early sixties, like me, but right behind him is a woman about the same age; must be his wife. Well I'm comfortable with that. No problems with a husband and wife as neighbours, maybe even new friends. Can't have too many of those. Maybe I could take a banana loaf over later when their moving truck leaves. I'm planning to do some baking this morning anyway; I'll just make an extra loaf. I would like to meet the people who will be living right across the street from me.

At about four in the afternoon, the moving truck having been gone for a couple of hours, I decided to go over to meet my new neighbours. I had better change out of these flour covered clothes before I go.

Knocking on the front door, I can hear the dog barking. In a few seconds the door opens and a woman is standing in the doorway.

"Hi I'm Maggie Henderson. I live across the street. I would just like to welcome you to the neighbourhood and offer you this banana bread I made this morning."

"Thank you Maggie. I'm Sheila Rogers. Please step inside and meet my husband Bill and this is our baby, Rufus. Sheila went on to explain that she is a retired nurse and Bill has just retired from a large engineering firm in Toronto. Bill was their computer analyst for the past eleven years. He's hoping to set up a small business, from home, helping people with their computers."

"I can tell you he will do well in this community. At our ages we weren't brought up with computers the way the kids are today. We have to learn rather than search and find as they do now."

"Nice to meet you both and Rufus. I won't stay, I know you're busy but maybe we can get together one day when you have settled in."

"I would love that. Could you fill us in on the activities here?"

"I would be happy to. See you later."

Well, they seem like very nice people. I'm glad I introduced myself and met them. I also recently met the widow who bought Gordon's house. She is very friendly but is still working full time so I don't see too much of her at the moment. Now I can feel comfortable with my surroundings.

As I open my eyes on Sunday morning, I'm feeling lost. Sunday used to be my favourite day. Joe and I would just relax over breakfast. We sipped our coffee, read the newspaper and just enjoyed each other's company. Again the tears start. I'm all alone now. What can I do today to keep myself busy? I hate Sundays now. Well get up, shower and have breakfast and maybe something will come to mind that I can do alone.

My self-pitying thoughts are interrupted by the phone.

"Hello."

"How are you, Mom?"

It is my daughter Pat.

"Just fine Dear and you?"

"I'm good too. Just want to invite you for a dinner tonight. Peter and Will are coming as well."

"That would be great. May I bring something?"

"No thanks Mom, I have it covered. Just be here around four and we can visit before dinner."

"Okay see you at four, and thanks."

I can always count on the kids to uplift my mood. Now today won't be so bad. I can work around the house knowing that I have a dinner date with my whole family.

As I arrive at Pat and James' house, I notice extra cars. Peter and Will are here but they didn't come together. That's a little strange.

Entering the house, I see a lovely young woman who I've never seen before. The kids all rush up to hug me and welcome me to the party. Then Will takes this pretty young woman by the hand and brings her to stand in front of me.

"Mom, I would like you to meet my girlfriend Emily Horton. Emily this is my Mom, Maggie."

"It's very nice to meet you Emily. Have you known Will very long?"

"Just a few months."

"Welcome to the party and I hope we see more of you in the future."

"Thank you Mrs. Henderson and it's a pleasure to meet you. Will talks about you all the time."

"Please call me Maggie. We're not formal in this family."

"Okay Maggie, thanks for welcoming me."

We had a delicious dinner that Pat had prepared for us all. I told the kids about Matt. I also told them that he was just a friend.

"Mom," Peter spoke up. "You deserve to be happy. Dad would have wanted you to have male friends or even more. Enjoy yourself."

"We agree," the others all chimed in.

I took a deep breath and I'm now much more at ease. I was worried how the kids might feel about my seeing someone, even as a friend.

"Would everyone like coffee with their dessert?"

A unanimous *yes* erupted. I'm pleased that everyone in my family enjoys their food. Pat is such a good cook. It would be a shame to turn her offer down. I had just taken the first sip of my coffee when Will spoke up.

"I had a reason for asking Pat to host this dinner tonight. Emily and I would like you to be the first to know that we are planning to get married as soon as possible."

Peter never was backward in coming forward and he quickly replied.

"Is there a pressing reason, Will?"

"As a matter of fact Peter, Emily is pregnant."

You could hear a pin drop in the room. Everyone is so quiet we just don't know what to say. I think I should break the silence and speak first.

"Will, you've shocked us all but I would like to welcome Emily into our family and I wish you all the best."

The others took my cue and also wished Will and Emily happiness.

"Emily, I would like to help you in any way I can. I hope the wedding will be in our church. Do you have a place in mind for a reception?"

"I have a few thoughts, but my parents don't know yet so I would like to tell them first and get back to you. Thanks for being so kind to me."

"Of course Emily, you are going to be a Henderson soon and we look after each other."

"Thanks, mom. Emily and I were worried about telling everyone tonight. I should have trusted that you would all be supportive, thanks."

"I love you Will and I will do whatever you need me to do."

A week later Emily and Will came to visit me for lunch.

"We told my parents that we are getting married. When I said I was pregnant my father hit the roof. He said he would never accept Will into our family. I was very upset and started crying. Will put his arm around my shoulder to comfort me. Then my mother came over and said she would speak to my dad to try to make him understand that the wedding was going to happen".

Mrs. Horton did speak to him and he promised not to cause any trouble at the wedding but he still was not happy.

My parents have offered to pay for the reception but they don't have a venue in mind that we could reserve on such short notice."

"Let me show you our community hall. If you like it, I'm sure I could reserve it for the reception. There would be no charge to me as a resident. All that your parents would be responsible for would be the food and drink. I could look after the music and a photographer if you wish."

After lunch we walked over to the hall. Emily and Will thought it was perfect so I offered to book it for them.

"Emily, I would like to throw a shower for you but since we have such short notice, could you give me a list of your friends and family members whom you would like me to invite and I'll send the invitations via e-mail. We could have it here at my house in two weeks."

"Okay thanks, I'll do that as soon as I get home this afternoon."

Later that day I am going through everything in my mind and the phone rings.

"Hello"

"Hello, is that Maggie Henderson?"

"Yes, may I help you?"

"This is Amanda Horton, Emily's mother. My husband and I would like to invite you and your friend, if you wish, to come to our house for dessert and coffee next Saturday evening. We want to meet you and I think we have a lot to discuss and plan and very little time to do it."

"Thank you Amanda. I'll ask Matt if he would like to join us but either way I would be happy to come."

I'll ask Matt tonight when we go walking. We are becoming quite the walking duo and we both have noticed a big difference in how we are feeling. At my last doctor's appointment my blood pressure had returned to normal. I guess it was all the stress I was under. Now I am walking every day and having the occasional dinner with my friend Matt and my work situation has been simplified. A lot of the pressure that I was feeling has been removed. Walking every evening with Matt is an unexpected plus. It's five to seven. I better get outside. We meet at seven at the corner of the street.

As I am walking close to Matt's house I hear:

"Good evening Maggie."

"Good evening yourself, Matt. How are you tonight?"

"Just fine Maggie and you?"

"I'm good but I have something to ask you. Please don't feel obligated, you can say no."

"Now you're scaring me. Just ask."

"I told you about my son getting married. Well the bride's parents have invited me for coffee and dessert on Saturday evening and they also invited you. Would you like to accompany me?"

"Maggie, I would be honoured and I'm glad you are asking me."

When Saturday evening came, Matt and I went to the Horton's home. We were able to iron out a lot of the details of the wedding.

"It is my pleasure to help with some of the arrangements. The hall for the reception is booked for us. I have arranged for the music and photographer. I also reserved the church for 4 o'clock in the afternoon. It is reserved for two Saturdays from now. Is there anything else I can do?"

"Could you help me address the invitations? I want to get them in the mail tomorrow morning."

"Sure I could help with that right now and get it out of the way."

On the way home, Matt was quite talkative saying how delighted he was to be part of this occasion.

"Matt, would you be my escort to the rehearsal dinner and the wedding? I would love to have you there with me."

"Maggie nothing would please me more, thank you."

Matt walked me to my door and he leaned in for a good night kiss. This time I didn't turn my cheek. I welcomed his lips on mine.

"Matt this feels so right but why do I feel like I am cheating on Joe?"

"Maggie I feel that way too but we're not cheating and I know our late spouses would want us to enjoy life."

Oh Matt, I am starting to develop feelings that I never expected to feel again. Should I break it off now or continue. If I stay, I know it will lead to something stronger and I'm not sure I'm ready for that. I don't know how

Matt feels about me. He is always so polite, I can't read him. I still get a very strong feeling that there is more to his story that he's not telling me. I give him one more kiss and say good night. He kisses me back but seems quite happy to leave.

Chapter 17

The bridal shower went off without a hitch. Twenty two ladies came and the kids got some lovely gifts. Everyone enjoyed the party and the food that Joan and I prepared.

Next Friday is the rehearsal dinner. Matt is accompanying me and I hope I can get him to open up. I feel he's keeping something from me and it could be important. I'm feeling much closer to him than I want to and I just have to find out what he is hiding.

The rehearsal dinner is at a local hotel and the food is superior. It's a buffet and I'm sure the Horton's spared no expense on the spread. There's just about everything you could imagine from meat to fish to pasta. The desserts are to die for. It's a great party but we should leave early because tomorrow is the wedding and it will be a very busy day.

Again Matt walks me to my door and again a good night kiss.

"Matt would you like to come in for a coffee."

"Just a very quick one because you need your rest. Tomorrow's a big day."

Well at least he accepted my invitation but I still have that funny feeling. I'm going to try to get him to talk.

"Come into the kitchen and take a seat. I'll put the coffee maker on; it only takes a couple of minutes. Maybe we can talk while we're waiting."

"Okay, any specific topic?"

"I want to know all about you Matt. I think there is more to you than you have told me."

"Maggie I've told you everything, I don't know what else you want to know."

"Nothing I guess," I lied. The more I talk to Matt the more I feel I'm right. What is his secret? I'm falling for this man and I'm afraid his secret may hurt me. Maybe I should just end it after Will's wedding. It breaks my heart to think this way as I feel Matt is a good man but I can't deal with secrets.

After our coffee, we kiss again only this time much stronger and with a heart-warming hug and then good night.

I feel frustrated like I can't get into his heart. What can I do? Well for now I should go to bed as I have to be alert for Will's big day tomorrow.

The church is decorated with flowers and Emily and Will are saying their vows in front of fifty friends and family members. It's a beautiful wedding and the bride looks stunning, maybe some of that is the pregnancy glow she has but nevertheless she is lovely. My new daughter-in-law.

At the reception, we enjoyed a delicious meal prepared by a local catering service that I have used before, when Joe was alive.

It is time for the speeches and we are all holding our breath as Emily's dad stands up. He surprised everyone by welcoming Will into the family but not before he stated his opinion.

We are dancing and making the rounds to talk to our guests. It's a beautiful wedding. I'm feeling very close to Matt as we dance around the floor. I know I've had a couple of drinks but I just have to be honest with Matt so I swallow my pride and try to stop shaking and I foolishly say:

"Matt, I think I'm falling in love with you."

The silence was deafening and then he replied but not how I expected him to reply. He simply said:

"Thank you."

I wish the floor would open up and swallow me right now. I'm so embarrassed. Why did he respond so calmly? I just declared my love for him and he as much as brushed me off. What's wrong with me?

Now we are on the way home and I don't know what to expect. Matt is as talkative as usual but I can't tell what he is thinking. At the door he asks:

"Could I come in for a minute or two?"

Boy now I'm really worried; maybe he is breaking off with me.

"Sure." I'm so scared this was all I could say. Not too intelligent but if I tried to say more I'm sure I would burst out crying, so better keep quiet.

Once inside the house Matt takes me in his arms. The kisses and hugs were terrific but still no "I love you." What's going on here? I guess he doesn't have the same feelings that I do but his kisses say otherwise. What should I do?

Matt only stayed a few minutes as we were both tired.

It's two in the morning and I'm still awake staring at the ceiling. I can't take any more of this lying awake nonsense. Tomorrow I'm going to end it with Matt. I feel bad doing this but it is for my own protection. Matt is keeping a secret from me and he's not forthcoming so I'm out of this relationship.

I finally fell asleep around four thirty, I think, so I am sleeping in this morning. At least that was my plan until the phone rang at nine fifteen.

"Hello," I answered sleepily.

"Good morning Maggie." It was Matt and he wants to come over to talk.

"Matt, just give me an hour to shower and dress and come for breakfast. I would like to talk to you too."

I'm going to tell him that it's over between us. It just isn't something I am looking for right now. I have had enough disappointment and heartache to last a lifetime. I certainly don't need more.

The coffee is on and the coffee cake is in the oven warming up when the doorbell rings. I'm so nervous I can hardly walk to the door. What will his reaction be to my decision? Maybe he is coming over to tell me the same thing. He certainly doesn't love me; that much I know.

When I open the door, I'm taken back by how handsome Matt looks in his jeans and white sweater. This is going to be sooo difficult, breaking it off with such a beautiful man.

"Please come in."

"Thanks for letting me intrude on your Sunday like this but there's something I must talk to you about."

"I want to talk to you too."

"Do you mind if I speak first Maggie? This is very difficult for me and if I don't get it out I might change my mind."

"I heard what you said at the wedding and I know I wasn't very responsive. I'm sorry about that."

I'm shaking; here comes the breakup. Oh I hope I don't start crying again. I just have to stay strong because if he breaks up with me I won't have to do it. That doesn't make me feel any better so let's just get it over with so I can carry on with my life.

"As I was saying, this is very difficult for me. I swore I would never be this vulnerable again. Let me explain:

A couple of years after my wife passed away, I met Julia at a social coffee hour after church. Once a month we used to meet in the church basement for coffee and goodies after the service. We started going out as friends, as you and I have been doing, and it progressed to dinners and we started dating. We fell in love, or so I thought. I had my life all planned with Julia as my wife. I decided to ask her to marry me and that is when I saw her with another man. The day I was going to propose to her, I was walking to the corner store and I saw her in the coffee shop with a stranger. At least he was a stranger to me. They were holding hands and staring into each other's eyes. I rushed home thinking my eyes had deceived me and maybe it was just a friend. Julia and I had a date for dinner later that evening and I was intending to propose to her. I went to pick her up and before we left the house I asked her who accompanied her for coffee that morning. She was very surprised because she had no idea that she had been spotted. Because I had seen them she had to tell me. Julia said she met this man two months ago and they had been seeing a lot of each other. Julia said she was falling in love with him. I couldn't believe what I was hearing. We talked for a few minutes and then I left, never telling her of my intention to propose.

I spent the next six months very depressed. How could I be so wrong about someone I cared for so much? As I cried myself to sleep most nights, and, yes, men do cry, I made a vow to never be that vulnerable again. Then I met you, Maggie.

We started out as friends after your loss and I was more than happy to comply. I had no intention of getting serious with anyone, ever again. But as time went on we seemed to be getting closer and closer. I have been fighting my feelings for you with everything that is in me. I don't want to repeat what happened with Julia. I'm telling you this now because I'm going up north to close my cottage for the season and I would like to invite you to accompany me. I want you to know the whole truth about me before you make up your mind to accept or decline my invitation.

I know how you feel and I feel guilty for not responding as I should have when you declared your feelings. I'm truly sorry. Maybe with a week at the cottage together we can see if there is anything between us or if we are to remain friends."

I had no idea that Matt was so torn up and confused. I really do like him and, yes, I think I'm falling in love with him but I certainly don't want to hurt him any more than he has already been hurt. I think a week away would help us to get to know each other and I'd like to know more about Matt. My heart is also very fragile at this point in time. I hope I'm not making a mistake.

"Okay Matt, I would love to accept your invitation for a week away and to explore our feelings toward each other. Like you, I don't want to jump into something and then get hurt. Let's just take things very slowly."

"Maggie that sounds great. Can you go next week?"

"I would prefer the week after next because I have an appointment with my ophthalmologist and I have waited three months for it. Would that work for you?"

"Yes we can leave on Saturday morning. It's about a three hour drive so that way we should be there by lunch."

"I'll be ready by nine."

"Good, I'll pick you up. Just bring your clothes and personal items. I'll take care of the food."

"Thanks Matt, I look forward to our time away together."

"Now that I have taken up so much time with my problems, what did you want to say?"

"Oh, nothing now. You answered all my questions." Boy, I feel lucky. I was planning to break it off with Matt before he explained his circumstance. Now I would like to give us a chance. We seem so similar, both of us have had our hearts broken and we are extremely fragile.

Chapter 18

I didn't sleep very well last night. This is the morning I have promised to go away with Matt for a week to his cottage. "Oh my darling Joe, what do you think about this?" I'm pretty sure you would tell me to enjoy myself but I feel guilty just trying to be happy without you. Well, better get up and get showered and dressed. I told Matt I would be ready at nine. My knees are weak and my heart is skipping the odd beat, I am so nervous. What have I done this time?

An hour later I am dressed and packed. At five minutes before nine I hear a knock on the front door.

"Good morning Matt."

"Good morning, are you all packed and ready?"

"Yes." I answered his question very sheepishly as I'm still unsure about this trip.

"I'll take your suitcase to the car while you lock up the house."

We drove the three hours to Huntsville where Matt has a cottage. As we were driving past all the little shops on the main street Matt suggested:

"I thought we could stop for lunch before continuing on to the cottage. What do you think?"

"I'd like that, I'm getting pretty hungry."

We drove over a small bridge and Matt turned left into one of my favourite restaurant chains. This restaurant is on the water with a lovely patio where we were lucky enough to get a table.

"Matt, this is beautiful. Thanks for bringing me here." The weather was perfect; sunny and about twenty five degrees Celsius or eighty degrees Fahrenheit. As we sat on the patio, we watched a few small boats travelling along the waterway. I felt so happy and peaceful. I haven't had a feeling like this since before Joe died. It feels wonderful.

"You're welcome. Would you like to share a pizza?"

"That would be perfect." Matt ordered a large Tuscan pizza and two light beers and we enjoyed our lunch.

"We are about fifteen minutes from my cottage. I thought we could spend the afternoon just relaxing, unpacking and I could show you around the area near the cottage."

"That would be lovely. I look forward to a walk to stretch my legs after our long ride."

"There are some very nice trails around my cottage and I would be happy to show you a couple today."

We put the groceries away first.

"Maggie, your bedroom is at the top of the stairs. There's a bathroom right beside it and that will be yours. My room is down here. I'll carry your suitcase up the stairs for you. Let me know if you need anything. There are towels and blankets in the bathroom closet."

"Thanks Matt."

I changed from the shorts I was wearing into jeans because mosquitoes seem to really like me. I can't wear a long sleeved top because it's still very warm so I'll put on lots of insect repellent. I brought a new bottle of repellent and a new sunscreen 30 SPF. I think today calls for the bug stuff as we will be under trees and shade. I also brought a hat for the sun but today I'm using it to keep bugs out of my hair. I had a June bug caught in my pony tail when I was young and I have never forgotten the terror I felt until someone removed it. I no longer have the pony tail but I do have hair and I'm going to cover it just in case. Now put on my sneakers and away I go.

We started out to the right of the cottage, along the water's edge. There was a path going up through the trees and Matt said this was a superb trail so we headed up the path. We walked for about an hour when the trail took a turn and we headed back towards the cottage. We walked for almost two hours and when we arrived back home we were so tired that we just fell into the deck chairs that were on the beach.

"Let's rest for a little while and then I'll start the barbeque."

"That's great Matt. What can I do to help?"

"After our rest you could make a salad, I have all the ingredients in the kitchen. While you are doing that, I'll cook two sirloin steaks."

"Sounds perfect, now let's just enjoy looking at the water."

I must have fallen asleep because the next thing I knew, the sun was gone and I was starting to feel chilly. I sat up and looked around. No Matt in sight. Where could he be? How long was I asleep? Just then Matt came up the beach.

"Have a nice rest, Maggie?"

"Yes, I think I fell asleep."

"You did for about an hour. You looked so peaceful I didn't want to disturb you so I just went for a walk along the beach."

I am so embarrassed. What kind of guest am I?

"Thanks for letting me sleep. I guess I was tired out after our hike."

"The fresh air up here will get you for a couple of days, until you get used to it."

"Okay Matt, let's start dinner."

"The barbeque is on and ready for the steaks. By the time you have a salad made, they will be ready and we can eat."

"Cheers Maggie." Matt toasted with a glass of red wine.

"Cheers to our friendship and a good week," I responded making sure I dropped the friendship card. No hanky panky on my agenda.

We enjoyed our dinner and afterwards Matt suggested a game of cards. He taught me a new game that could easily be played by two and we played until the wee hours of the morning. When we were both having trouble keeping our eyes open we retired to our own rooms for the night.

The next morning I awoke to the sounds of birds singing. This is a wonderful feeling waking up this way. I don't know what we are doing today so I'll just put on my robe and go downstairs for breakfast. I can start the coffee. I don't know yet what Matt likes for breakfast so I'll just wait for him.

I was drinking my first cup of coffee when Matt came into the kitchen.

"The wonderful aroma of coffee woke me this morning. Thank you Maggie."

"You're welcome. What would you like for breakfast?"

"Whatever you normally have is fine for me."

"Then toast, juice and coffee it is."

"I have to go into town this morning to get a new hinge for the closet in my bedroom. The door sticks and I have trouble opening it so I want to replace the hinge. Would you like to join me? There are some very nice, small stores on the main street and we could look around them for a while if you like."

"Oh yes, I love browsing in boutiques. Can you give me an hour to shower and dress?"

"Maggie, we are on vacation. Take all the time you need. I will be outside weeding the garden in the front of the cottage."

On the way into town Matt was very talkative again. He seemed exceptionally happy. We seem to be getting along well together as friends and I wonder if our friendship could possibly develop into more. I'm being very cautious and I can tell Matt is doing the same. Both of us protecting our feelings. I guess we both have to learn to trust.

"There's a parking lot just behind these stores so I'll park here and we can walk to the hardware store across the street."

"Okay Matt, I'll go with you to the hardware store before we check out the boutiques."

As soon as we walked through the door a very attractive woman ran up to Matt and threw her arms around his neck and gave him a kiss on the cheek.

"Matty how long has it been? I've missed seeing you up here at the lake."

I feel out of place. Who is this woman? She certainly likes Matt. Wait a minute here comes a man.

"Matt, it's nice to see you. I see my wife has already welcomed you back."

"How are you Bob? And Linda it's nice to see you too. This is my friend Maggie. We're at the cottage for a week's vacation."

"Nice to meet you Maggie, I'm Linda. We have the white cottage just down the beach from Matt's. Hope you enjoy your week."

"Hey Matty, we are having a few neighbours over for a bonfire on the beach tonight. Why don't you come and bring Maggie?"

"Maggie would you like to go to their bonfire tonight. We could just walk down the beach. It's less than five minutes away from my cottage."

"I'd love that. I've never been to a bonfire. What can we bring?"

"A bottle of whatever you like to drink would be great. See you at nine."

"Thanks Bob, nice to see you again," Matt called after them as they left the store.

Wow! This trip is turning out to be fun. I thought we'd just be sitting around making small talk for a week. I think when we go into the stores I'll see if I can get a warm sweatshirt. I didn't bring anything warm enough to sit on the beach at night. Good, now I have a reason to shop.

I managed to get a nice, warm, pink sweatshirt.

"Would you like a hot dog in the park? Matt suggested. It's getting close to lunchtime and we haven't seen all the stores yet. We can put your package in the car and start again after lunch."

"That sounds good. I'm hungry too."

We ate our hot dogs and shared a bottle of water and then headed back to the shops. After a couple of hours we returned to the car to go back to the cottage. We spent the rest of the afternoon lying on the beach in our bathing suits and getting some sun.

After dinner Matt and I both donned our jeans and warm sweatshirts. It gets cool by the water once the sun goes down. We took a bottle of red wine from the wine rack in the kitchen and headed down the beach to Bob and Linda's cottage. The fire was already lit in a very elaborate black iron stove. Half a dozen people huddled around the fire.

"Welcome Matt and Maggie. Come and meet our neighbours, Maggie. Matt I think you know everyone."

"It's been a couple of months since I have been up here. What's new? Have I missed anything important?"

"Not much. The couple in the green cottage at the end of the beach just got divorced."

"That's not surprising. They were fighting the last time I was up here."

"Everything else seems to be status quo, I think."

"Incidentally, I approve of your new girlfriend," Bob remarked.

"Oh no! Maggie and I are just friends and neighbours."

"Matt, I see the way you look at each other and you are more than friends."

"Well maybe someday but we're taking our time. We've both suffered losses and we need to be careful this time. We need time to heal."

"Well good luck with that one. I think you may have passed careful a while back."

The rest of our week was quiet and uneventful but a very welcomed rest. We stuck to our promise and just remained friends without benefits.

Chapter 19

It's Sunday again and I am at home on the computer. Dr. John is giving a speech tomorrow and he asked me to type up his notes. I'm about half way through this work when the power suddenly cuts out. The lights have gone off and all the clocks in my house have stopped. About two minutes later the power has returned. I guess I'll fix the clocks later. This work is very important but, Oh shit! Where is my work? I've been saving it as I go along but where on earth has it gone. I'll try looking at different documents. I can't find it. My temper is rising. I hate computers and their problems. I don't know enough about them to find anything. As long as everything goes my way I'm happy but glitches are not my friends. Oh! I just want to throw this *damn* computer out the window. Okay, I think I had better walk away for a few minutes. I'll just fix the clocks and maybe I'll come up with a solution. Shit! Shit! Shit! What can I do on Sunday with most computer stores closed? Why did I leave it to the last minute? Now I have a big problem.

Wait a minute now, my new neighbour is a computer technician. Oh I hope he's home. As I make the call, my fingers are crossed that he can help me but after five rings I guess he isn't home. I'll just push keys and see if I can fix it. Ha ha ha. That isn't likely to happen. After ten minutes of my foolishly pushing keys the phone rings.

"Hello."

"Hello Maggie this is Bill returning your call. I was in the shower when you called, sorry. What can I do for you?"

"Well Bill, thanks for returning my call. I'm having problems with my computer. The power went out briefly and I lost a very important document. Could you help me find it?"

"I'll try. Be right over."

"Bill, bring Sheila. I have a pot of coffee on and we can visit when you're finished with my computer."

"Thanks Maggie. Sheila is downstairs working on a sewing project but I'll ask her if she can take a break."

A few minutes later Bill and Sheila arrived at my door.

"Please come in. Sheila it's nice to see you. Just take a seat in the kitchen and I will be with you as soon as I show Bill the computer."

Bill is very knowledgeable on the computer and it didn't take long before he had retrieved my work.

"Thanks Bill. Now would you like to join Sheila and me in the kitchen for coffee?"

As we sat with coffee and cinnamon rolls fresh from the oven, I learned that Sheila and Bill did not have a traditional marriage. It seems they both go their own way. They live together amicably but date other people. I don't understand this arrangement; but to each his own.

"Maggie, could you explain some of the activities to us?" Sheila asked.

"Sure what are you interested in? We have all the usual outdoor games, for example golf and tennis. We also have line dancing, knitting, painting and stained glass, pool, wood carving. Actually my late husband Joe made that horse on the mantel at a wood carving class. He really enjoyed that class. Oh and Sheila, we have a ladies social group here. We meet once a month and plan outings together such as day trips, shows, lunches and many other things. There's a meeting in two weeks on Monday morning. If you'd like to go, you could join Sue, Barb and me."

"Thank you I'd love to go. I want to meet some more of our neighbours."

After one and a half hours of visiting, Bill and Sheila went back home and I got back to my work at the computer. Everything went well with no more power outages.

Chapter 20

Today is going to drag. I have a dinner date with Matt and I'm really looking forward to it. Matt and I have been going out for dinner about three times a week. We don't always go to a fancy restaurant. Sometimes we just go to the local burger place. They have a light choice on their menu; chicken burger with a salad. I quite often order this. It's not much fun cooking for one and even less fun eating alone, so Matt and I have been going out to eat before our evening walks. Can't wait for tonight. We are still friends without benefits but it still feels right. I enjoy Matt's company and I know he likes to be with me. Matt is not fluent with romantic words and he still hasn't said "I love you" but I know by his actions that he is at least interested in me. I wish he could find the words to tell me how he feels.

Today is a short day at the office, so I think I will visit Joe at the cemetery on my way home. I go there sometimes just to be quiet and think. I also like to talk to Joe when something is bothering me. It seems I find the answer I'm looking for. I do believe that Joe is watching over me and helping me find solutions to my problems.

As I drive in through the large iron gates and straight along the same road, I come to the wall of niches were Joe's ashes are residing. I'll just park the car close and get out to talk to Joe.

"Hi, my darling Joe. It's me again with another dilemma. I'm sure you are watching over me and you would want me to be happy. I have been seeing a man named Matt and we are very compatible. Joe, you are and always will be the love of my life but you're gone now and I am here alone. I have fallen for Matt in a big way. I'm troubled because he doesn't seem to share my feelings. When we are together he is wonderful. He holds my hand, puts his arm around my shoulder and kisses me with immense passion but he has never said "I love you". I'm worried that I might get my heart broken. We have another date tonight and I really look forward to these dates. I hope Matt does as well.

Thanks again Joe for listening to my problems. I always feel better when I can talk to you, my forever love."

It's six o'clock and I'm wearing my jeans and a sweater. Matt and I decided tonight would be a casual night. We are going for fish and chips and then coming home for our walk. I am starting to feel very comfortable with our arrangement.

The doorbell rings and it's Matt also wearing jeans and a sweater.

"Hi Matt I'm all ready to go and very hungry."

"Me too Maggie. Let's go."

The waitress took our order and I asked for my favourite halibut and chips with coleslaw on the side. Matt ordered the same but he asked for two pieces of fish. We talked all through the meal and the coffee following our dinner. I can't believe how comfortable I feel with Matt. I just wish he would give me some idea how he is feeling. I've already declared my feelings to him so all I can do is wait and pray.

After dinner we drove home.

"I'll just grab my jacket and meet you outside in five minutes," I said.

"Okay Dear, I'll be at your driveway in five minutes."

My heart is beating extra fast. Matt finally called me Dear. Does this mean he is falling for me or is it just a polite habit?

"Hi Matt, I'm ready to walk."

"Hi Maggie," Matt said as he took my hand.

We walked hand in hand for an hour and then when we arrived at my house, I asked Matt in for a drink.

"I'd love to come in for a drink but only for a short time; it's getting late."

"Would you like wine?"

"Yes, thanks."

"I have red and white and I also have peach coolers."

I'd like red wine. Let me open it and pour. What would you like?"

"I'll take red as well."

We sipped our wine while sitting in front of the fireplace and we were very comfortable with each other. I hoped Matt would loosen up and tell me how he feels. I kissed him and he kissed me back but still said nothing. Finally he got up and said he had to leave. I don't understand. I have never experienced this before and I don't know how to react. We kissed at the door but then he was gone.

Chapter 21

Today is my birthday and I'm sixty four. Matt has arranged to take me downtown to see a performance by The Four Tenors, a group we both love. They are all so talented and sing beautifully. Before the show we are having dinner. Matt has booked a private table in a large hotel near the theatre. I'm going to spend my day at the spa so I will look and feel terrific for tonight. I've chosen a lovely red dress with black patent heels to wear tonight. I want a sexy look for my birthday. After all, I can't look sixty four.

I'm feeling wonderful as I wait for Matt to come to the door. I really hope he lets me know how he feels about me tonight. I'm getting tired of waiting for confirmation of his love. He seems to be in love with me. His kisses are so very passionate and his hugs are wonderful but that's as far as it goes. Is he still afraid of getting hurt or is it that he's not that interested in me? I really need to know. All I think about these days is Matt but he hasn't reciprocated in the way I need. The doorbell rings and my heart skips a beat. I open the door and there stands my date. Matt is wearing a three piece navy suit and white shirt; he looks like he is going to a wedding. I'm a pushover for a man in a three piece suit. My heart skips another beat. Boy! At this rate I won't last the evening.

"Happy Birthday Maggie. You look fantastic tonight."

"Thanks Matt. You look pretty hot yourself."

We arrived at the restaurant and were seated at our private table in the back corner. There were three large green ferns surrounding our area. Matt ordered a bottle of wine and when it arrived he reached across the table and took my hand. He has to be the most romantic man.

"Cheers Maggie and Happy Birthday."

"Cheers."

As we were drinking our wine and talking, Matt reached into his jacket pocket and took out a small box from a jewellery store. My already nervous heart started to race. What could it be?

"Maggie, I bought you a small gift for your birthday. Hope you like it."

"Matt you shouldn't have. The dinner and show were more than enough."

"Please open it. When I saw it, I thought of you and so I bought it."

My fingers were shaking so much that I could barely unwrap it but I managed. Inside the wrapping was a purple velvet box. Now I'm even more nervous. I opened the box and inside was the prettiest ruby necklace I have ever seen. It was a small oval stone with tiny diamonds all around it.

"Oh! Matt this is beautiful but far too extravagant."

"Maggie, just say thank you and let me put it on you. It will look lovely with your red dress."

"Thank you Matt and it does look beautiful."

We finished our dinner and coffee in plenty of time to get to the show.

Listening to the tenors gives me goosebumps and always puts me in a romantic mood. I think they affect Matt in a similar way as he is squeezing my hand and touching my leg with his own. At intermission, we went to the lobby for a glass of wine. I'm starting to feel a little giddy with all the wine but Matt seems to be okay. When the show ended we had to walk back to the hotel where we had left the car. We held hands all the way back and I felt a few squeezes on the way.

"Maggie, how would you like to stay here at the hotel with me tonight and return home in the morning?"

This being my birthday, I was feeling very brave and maybe a little drunk so:

"I think that would be nice. It's a great birthday treat."

Matt put his arm around me as we headed up to the reception desk to book a room. I felt a little strange with no suitcases but Matt had that covered.

"We would like a room for the night please. We've just come from the show and we were both drinking so we don't want to drive home."

"We can sit by the fire for a while, have a drink, probably coffee since we have had enough wine tonight, and we can talk for a while."

"That sounds great but I think we should make the coffee decaf if we intend to sleep tonight."

We sat for an hour enjoying our coffee and talking. We discussed our choices in music, movies and other forms of entertainment. It seems that Matt and I enjoy a lot of the same things except for hockey. Matt likes to watch hockey but I find it boring.

I keep glancing nervously at the bed. What is going to happen at bedtime? I've been trying to stall for time. I'm sure Matt has some ideas or he wouldn't have asked me to stay in this hotel room with him. I think I'm ready but only time will tell.

"Maggie, you are a beautiful woman and I've been dreaming about a night like this for a long time now. If it is still too soon for you, I understand."

"Matt, I too have been dreaming and I want to give myself to you. I only hope it will happen for me."

We kissed and hugged and it was wonderful. Eventually we ended up in bed in each other's arms. I guess it was meant to be because neither of us had any trouble as we became one with each other.

The next morning we shared breakfast in the hotel restaurant before we headed back to our respective homes.

On the drive home we talked and laughed, just like old friends. I can't believe how content I feel with Matt. I am once more excited about the future. I can picture taking trips with Matt or just ordinary living. Holidays, which I usually dread, will be fun once more.

I look forward to my life now that we are more than just friends.

Author of:

Over 50

Perseverance

Watch for "over 60"

The second book in this trilogy

Fall/2016

Printed in the United States
By Bookmasters